MURDER ON THE LAKE
A VIKING WITCH COZY MYSTERY

CATE MARTIN

Cover design by Shezaad Sudar.

Ratatoskr Press logo by Aidan Vincent.

ISBN 978-1-951439-51-4

❀ Created with Vellum

CHAPTER 1

This was going to be the last halfway warm day of the year, I just knew it. I could feel it in my bones. So instead of heading straight inside the meeting hall to find my grandmother as I was supposed to, I veered instead off towards the bank of the river. It was the best place I'd found so far to sense the magic of the world around me, but soon it would be too cold to sit there for more than a minute or two.

I was early to meet my grandmother anyway, and the sun was going to sink under the western hills soon enough. I could take a moment to bask.

Not that it was warm enough for sunbathing or anything. I was wearing a windbreaker over my hoodie for a reason, and the brisk breeze that had nipped at my cheeks from the minute I had stepped out of my grandmother's cabin was even brisker when I approached the water. But any Minnesotan knows to make the most of Indian summer, because winter is never far behind.

I found my favorite flat boulder, high enough over the river so I didn't catch any of the spray from the water churning over the rocks below, but not so high that I couldn't hear that churning water's song. I sat down, crossed my legs, and closed my eyes.

1

The sun on my face felt warmer, although I could still feel the breeze twisting through my loose hair. It glowed redly through my eyelids, especially when I turned my face up to drink it in.

The smell of dried leaves slowly turning to dust filled the air. They had all lost their color some time ago, and there had been no rain in weeks, so they just covered the ground in a dusty, dry blanket. There was something to the smell, like a longing for that rain. Was there an opposite to the word petrichor? Because that felt like what I was smelling.

That, plus a hint of something else. Something like ozone after a lightning strike, but very faint, as if from long ago and far away. It eluded me when I tried to pinpoint it, but when I focused instead on the leaves around me it sneaked back into my perceptions.

Rather like the sounds of trucks passing on the highway bridge overhead, barely discernible over the sounds of the river before me, very easily ignored. Most days it was easier to hear the lake from where I was sitting, but not today. The breeze playing through my hair had no interest in stirring up that still water. Only the smallest of waves marred its dark gray surface.

But that wouldn't last. I could feel a pressure in the air, like something was building. Like a storm was brewing, although the skies were as calm as the water for as far as could be seen from the shore.

I had mentioned this feeling to my grandmother just that morning, and she had laughed it off. Storms didn't brew over the lake and then blow ashore; they came in from the west, from over land.

I supposed she was right. She had lived here all her life, after all. But still, there was a pressure against my eardrums that had been building all day. Something was about to happen. Something was about to change.

Without consciously deciding this was the moment to do so, I sank into a deeper state. The cold of the stone beneath me faded away, as did the sounds from the river. The red of the sunlight against my eyelids became something else, a ghostly tracing of forms around me. The trees on the bank on the far side of the river. The fish darting between the rocks below me.

After weeks and weeks of working so hard to master this skill, it was easy now, as automatic as smelling the leaves in the air. It was just there, this whole magical world. Once I had glimpsed it, it had become a part of me. Every living thing was something golden and beautiful, because every living thing had something of magic within it.

The bridge above me and the cars and trucks it carried over our little lakeside village didn't show up, save for the little magical glow from the humans and occasional live cargo they contained. In this state, it was as if I were sitting on the riverbank as it had existed for all the centuries before people had settled here. Just me and life itself.

But there was a brighter glow from behind me that bathed everything around me. This was entirely people-made and the strongest magic of all: the Runde meeting hall, soon to be transformed into the mead hall that served Runde and Villmark both. The only thing I had yet seen that held more magic was the sacred fire in the cave behind the waterfall. The fire that my ancestress Torfa had created centuries before.

That fire generated its own magic now through a means even my grandmother didn't understand. But the meeting hall did not. That had to be renewed, the spells recast every day at sunset.

I felt a shiver dance up my spine, and the wind in my hair had a decided chill to it now. I blinked away the magical tracings, found the more mundane red glow no longer shining through my eyelids, and opened my eyes to see the sun had gone down behind the hills.

Time to help my grandmother recast those spells.

I got up from the rock, dusted off the back of my jeans, and headed back up the narrow path from the river bank to the empty meeting hall parking lot.

The meeting hall was a drab place during the day. The old tables were all off-balance, tipping under any weight at all, and every chair sported multiple duct tape repairs, holding the plastic seats together over the scant padding. Brown water stains of various sizes marred the ceiling tiles above, and the light fixtures were equipped with the most horrific of fluorescent bulbs, bathing everything in a sickly greenish-yellow light. I would be hard-pressed to imagine a less welcoming-looking place if I tried.

Somehow, the Halloween decorations that Michelle and Jessica had helped me hang earlier that afternoon just made it all look sadder. Like the grinning Jack-o'-lanterns and bright bundles of multicolored cobs of corn were just trying too hard. This was no place to throw a warm and festive party.

"Ready?" my grandmother asked me as I stepped up to her bar. She was sipping at a mug of what I guessed was hot cider. I could smell cinnamon and cloves.

"I still feel that storm brewing," I said. "You're sure there's nothing going on?"

"Weather has its own power," she said, then took one last sip before setting the mug aside. "It's not magic. Well, not usually. You're noticing it more because you're still new to this. Everything probably feels like it's shouting at you." She raised a questioning eyebrow, but I just shrugged. The only thing grabbing my attention lately was whatever was brewing just out of sight over the eastern horizon. "Definitely keep turning your attention to it when you're meditating. Knowing what you feel now and comparing that to what happens in the future, that's how you'll build the sort of experience I'm talking about."

"Makes sense," I said. "Should I be keeping a journal or something?"

My grandmother blinked at me in surprise. "Aren't you already?"

"What?" I asked. "You never told me to."

"No, I mean, you sketch in your book. I've seen you drawing multiple pages in a rush every time you go upstairs to your room after we meditate together," she said.

"I do," I said. "I guess that *is* a journal of sorts."

"For you, it's ideal. You are a more visual thinker. It suits you," she said.

"And you?" I asked. "Do you keep a journal?"

She gave me a sly grin, then tipped her head towards one of the cut-outs of a witch with HAPPY HALLOWEEN scrawled on a banner that rippled over her pointy boots. "A witch never tells all her secrets," she said. "Now, shall we?"

I nodded and headed to the center of the room. My grandmother could cast these spells from anywhere, but I still liked to feel centered first. It didn't matter much in the drab meeting hall, with each of the water-stained tiles much like the others in an endless grid overhead. But in the mead hall I would be in the center of the space, between the two long tables with their benches, equidistant between the roaring fire on the hearth to the north and the mountainous pyramid of beer barrels stacked against the southern wall.

The first spell changed the look of the space around us. It wasn't casting an illusion, though. Neither the meeting hall nor the mead hall was a mirage; they were both totally real and they both really existed in this spot where we were standing. I still couldn't quite wrap my head around that. The closest way to describe it is holding two over-lapping film negatives up to the light. By focusing on one or the other, it was just possible to tune out the other one, but they were both always there. Our spell was really just a way to make everyone who entered the hall focus on the same image.

Not everyone was affected the same. That had been the second mind-blowing thing my grandmother had dropped on me. The fact that some Villmarkers came down from their village to visit what looked to them like an ugly pre-fabbed pole barn several decades past its prime was hard enough to imagine. But as my grandmother said, they were looking for the exotic, and that was what their minds stubbornly insisted they see.

But the residents of Runde who also saw only the drab hall they knew from the daytime? What was the draw for them?

Just the beer and the company, my grandmother had said.

Not that it mattered much what the people of Runde saw when they came after dark, because the second layer of spells we worked together were spells of forgetting. No one in the modern world could be allowed to walk around remembering that the night before they had been in a Viking long house drinking with actual Vikings. Not if we were going to keep Villmark safe.

Keeping Villmark safe was the sworn duty of the volva. That was my grandmother's office currently, and someday it might be mine as well, so we put extra care into maintaining those spells. But still, it was a little sad. All of my Runde friends visited somewhere amazing on a regular basis, but aside from some vivid dreams, they never recalled it the next morning.

There were more spells after the forgetting layer was in place, but they were smaller. Spells to keep the cold and wind out and the warmth in, spells to keep the beer fresh and the barrels never-empty-ing, spells to keep violence at bay. Patrons might get annoyed with each other, but no disagreement ever came to blows, not when my grandmother was in charge.

At first my role in this casting had been more as an observer, but the last few nights my grandmother had passed more and more of the work over to me. I could feel her magic supporting me, like her hands over mine on the rolling pin when we had baked cookies together when I was a little girl.

I felt that support again as I wove the spells together, but then all of a sudden it was just gone. I wanted to open my eyes and make sure my grandmother was okay, but in my magical sight I could see the spells starting to pull apart, unravelling like a scrap of knitting.

I couldn't sense my grandmother, and that had never happened before. But I had to lunge for that spellwork first. We didn't cast spells anew in the evening. Everything we did built on what was already there. If I let it go now, years of work could be reduced to nothing. Decades, even. I had to hold it together, finish each spell off and ground it into the hall itself, before I could even think of turning my attention to my grandmother.

But the back of my mind was still capable of worrying. Even as I traced patterns with my hands, moving in the physical and the magical worlds at once because I was still too new at this to do it all in my head, I worried.

My grandmother was old, older than I knew. She was in amazing shape and looked like she could continue on until the end of time, but surely that wasn't really true. Someday even she would falter with age. But surely not today?

I double-checked all my work before finally opening my eyes, sucking in a breath as if coming up from a deep dive far under water.

And saw my grandmother standing there, as healthy as ever, grinning at me.

"That was a test?" I asked.

"That was a test," she agreed. She was looking around as if at the rafters that supported the thatched roof above us, but I knew she was really checking my spells.

"Did I pass?" I asked.

"Of course you passed," she said. "Look around you. Self-assess."

"Well, obviously," I said. Everything looked like it should, and I could feel the warmth of the fire at my back even halfway across the room. The air smelled of the beer that never washed out of the wood of the tables and floors, and faintly of roasted meat, although nothing was currently cooking. "I know I didn't fail, but how well did I do?"

My grandmother just tisked and turned to head back to her bar to check on her mead.

I wasn't fishing for compliments; I swear. Just a little bit of feedback, that was all I wanted.

But as usual with my grandmother, I had to get by without it. I hadn't failed. For now, that was good enough.

CHAPTER 2

The Halloween decorations had made the transition from Runde meeting hall to Villmark mead hall. I wasn't sure they would. Nothing else did, after all. The rickety tables were now solid wood, the battered chairs long benches, the stained ceiling tiles nowhere in sight. But orange and black streamers twisted from rafter to rafter, and the pillars spaced down the length of the room were festooned with bundles of dried wheat and corn tied with colored ribbons. Even the cut-outs of witches and Jack-o'-lanterns were there, hanging on threads from the underside of the thatched roof lost in the shadows above.

It was more than a little incongruous. The Villmarkers were aware of Halloween as a Runde holiday, but they had no version of it themselves. They had harvest festivals, but none on the last night of October. The grain harvest had been celebrated weeks before, and the festival connected to the fat cows and pigs and goats that weren't going to be kept over the winter was still a couple of weeks away. I wasn't sure what that would involve, aside from a lot of meat at the feast and, apparently, some sort of communal sausage-making.

Some magical traditions say that the veil between the living and the dead is thinnest on Halloween night, that magic is more powerful then, especially magic that draws from your ancestors. But the Vikings considered that veil to be thinner all winter long.

Which made sense. The island the original Villmarkers had hailed from was north of the Arctic Circle. There winter wasn't just cold, it was dark, one long night that went on for weeks. I imagined their first winter here on the North Shore had been a happy one. Sure, it was colder here, without the Gulf Stream bringing warm air up from the south, but at least the sun was always there. It might be impossible to see behind steely gray clouds for days and days, but you knew it was there, trying to reach you.

I was still admiring the decorations, sipping at a mug of mulled cider my grandmother had pressed into my hands, when the front door opened and Michelle and Jessica came inside. Jessica, wearing a gorgeous red hooded cloak and carrying a basket full of apples and bread rolls, was clearly Little Red Riding Hood. She usually kept her long blonde hair in a braided crown, a fancy way of keeping it out of her way while she worked in the café, but today she had left it in two braids that hung like pigtails, peeking out of the front of her hood.

I took a little longer to work out who Michelle was supposed to be. Her gown was all princess, sapphire blue with long, draping sleeves, but there were a lot of princesses. Then she turned to look back towards the door, and I saw the blonde wig she wore was so long it dragged on the ground behind her. Rapunzel, for sure.

Then Andrew came in behind them. He was wearing his usual jeans and fisherman's sweater, but a green Robin Hood cap with a long red feather tucked into its brim covered all but one forelock of his dark blond hair. Then he too turned to look back, and I saw he had a little bow and quiver of arrows strung across his back. A little incongruous with the sweater, maybe, but the bow looked like he'd carved it himself. And, knowing Andrew, he probably had.

And finally appearing in the doorway, in normal modern clothes, was Loke. I couldn't decide if this meant he never wore a costume, or if he always did. Just black pants and a black shirt with equally black shoes; it was a little hard to tell.

Perhaps I shouldn't have been surprised at his nondescript look.

Loke divided his time between the two worlds far more than I did. He was as likely to come in through the front door under his Runde guise called Luke as he was to come in through the back as Loke.

But I hadn't seen him much lately. He had promised me a visit to his house, to meet his sister, but I had stopped pressing him on setting a date and time for that event.

Something was on his mind, something he didn't want to share with me. I hoped if I didn't press that he would come around more, maybe decide to share what was bothering him with me, but so far that hadn't happened.

"Hey, Ingrid!" Michelle said. "Wow, this looks great!"

"I don't think I've ever seen it so festive," Andrew said.

"It's just a few decorations," I said, "and you guys did as much of that as I did."

"Really?" Jessica asked, looking up at a witch twisting in a current of warm air from the fire over her head. "I guess we did some of it, but there's something different, something more. You did something after we left here, didn't you?"

"Not much," I said, but I was distracted by Loke smothering a chuckle and looking away innocently when Andrew shot him a puzzled glance. At least Loke seemed to be in a better mood.

"Is there a bonfire out back?" Michelle asked.

"Of course," I said. I had paid particular attention to that area when weaving the cold-repelling spells so that the fire and the electric heaters that ringed the patio would have a chance against the cold October wind.

"Apple bobbing?" Jessica asked eagerly, and not for the first time. She was really into apple bobbing, apparently.

"You wanted to start with that?" I asked.

"It's not going to get any warmer," Andrew said and pretended to shiver. "Does anyone else feel like it's just about to snow? I swear we're going to have flakes before the weekend."

"Not according to the app on my phone," Michelle said, glancing at its screen before tucking it away in a pocket hidden inside her voluminous sleeve. "But yeah, let's get the 'plunging our faces into icy water' part of the evening out of the way first."

"Out of the way?" Jessica said. "Come on, you *love* bobbing for apples."

"I think you're remembering a much younger Michelle," her friend said. But she grabbed Jessica's hand to lead the way out the back door to the patio.

And I found myself momentarily alone with Andrew, whose dark blue eyes quickly darted away when I looked over at him. Had he just been staring at me?

"I didn't even think to wear a costume," I said, looking down at my jeans and sweater. There was still mud on my hiking boots from the river bank. Great.

"You look fantastic," Andrew said, perhaps a bit too forcefully. He flushed, then spoke in a more neutral tone. "I mean, I suppose you put a lot of time into all this." He waved his hands at the room around us, and I saw Loke behind him hiding another grin behind his hand. I narrowed my eyes at Loke, only for a split second but I knew he got the message. Then I looked back at Andrew.

"It's not much, really," I said.

He looked like he had no idea what to say to that. And that being tongue-tied was causing him real agony. But I didn't know what to say either. Why was this so suddenly awkward, talking to him?

"I was going to grab a beer. Did you want a beer?" he asked at last.

"No, I've got cider already," I said, although in truth my mug was nearly empty. "Meet you out back?"

"Sure thing," he said, then made his way to the beer barrels, already surrounded by a milling group of Villmarkers who had come in while my attention was on my Runde friends.

"You stop laughing," I hissed at Loke.

"Who, me?" he asked with feigned surprise. Then he gave me a conspiratorial look. "Come on, you have to see the humor. I mean, how much of this do they even really see?"

"All of it," I said, surprised that he didn't know that. "They just don't remember it."

"Really?" he said, looking around with his eyes slightly unfocused. "Oh. Yes, I see."

"Do you?" I asked.

"Would I lie to you?" he asked. "Everyone else, sure, if the situation called for it. Or if it seemed fun. But you?"

"I have no idea," I admitted. "You're in a strange mood."

He just shrugged, then nodded towards the back door. I walked with him out onto the patio. The wind immediately tossed my hair into my eyes, but it wasn't a cold wind. The warmth-containing spells had worked.

Jessica, her blindfold tied around her hooded head, was already bent over face-first into the barrel full of water and floating apples. The ends of both of her braids were getting soaked. Michelle was cheering her on, and so were Nilda and Kara, my closest Villmarker friends.

They were wearing their full armor, helms and all. They had dressed like this in the mead hall before, after our day out on the lake in the ship when everyone had worn their traditional garb, but unlike that time, the others seemed to notice it today. Two Runde fishermen standing by the bonfire were clearly impressed, trying to sneak closer glances at their swords.

"I think those are real," one whispered to the other.

"Hey, Ingrid!" Michelle said when I approached. "Aren't Nilda's and Kara's costumes amazing?"

"Indeed," I agreed, then to the two Villmarkers, "Happy Halloween."

"Happy Halloween," Nilda said. There was a slightly stilted quality to how she said it, like she was pronouncing a foreign word, although her English was otherwise flawless.

"Nilda," Kara said, nudging her sister's elbow, "let's grab some mead and come back out."

"Yeah," Nilda agreed, then smiled at me. "Be right back."

"Sure thing," I said. She had only made eye contact with me, and I realized Loke was no longer at my side. Where had he gone off to?

Michelle shrieked and danced back as a wave of water sloshed out of the barrel. Then Jessica straightened up, an apple grasped firmly in her teeth. It was a huge apple, but Jessica's smile was bigger. She pulled off the blindfold, then took the apple out of her mouth.

"Not exactly record time," she said, "but now it's your turn."

Michelle bit at her lip, clearly hoping to find the words to beg off, when another voice came to her rescue.

"May I have a try?"

Another Villmarker woman in full Viking armor had stepped out of the shadows beyond the end of the patio.

"Gullveig!" I said, recognizing Nilda's and Kara's friend. We had only met a few times before, and then only briefly, but she was impossible to mistake for any other. Tall even by Villmarker standards and basically made of supermodel material, she didn't need the sword at her hip to catch the attention of the Runde fishermen watching from the bonfire.

Michelle stepped back as Jessica tied the blindfold over Gullveig's eyes.

"You could just take an apple from that basket over there if you want," I said to Michelle as we watched Jessica guide the Villmarker closer to the barrel. "There's salted caramel in that fondue pot for dipping the slices in."

"That sounds divine," Michelle said and followed me to the picnic table under the eaves.

"How is Jessica doing?" I asked, pitching my voice a little lower, although I doubted Jessica could hear me over her own shrieks. Gullveig had thrust her head into the water so exuberantly the patio for feet around was soaked.

"She's good," Michelle said, but there was a false note to her voice. I raised my eyebrows at her. "Better than before," she amended. "She doesn't talk about Lisa as much as before, but I think she's still always thinking of her. Wondering what really happened to her."

"I guess that's to be expected," I said. "It's only been a few months." Still, it made my heart sank. I would give almost anything to be able to tell Jessica that her friend's murder *had* been solved, if not by the police. That the murderer had been caught and would never harm another again.

Almost anything, but not the one thing I would have to give up in order to tell her the truth. Because telling her that would mean telling her about Villmark, and that I could not do.

"Oh, dear," Michelle said with a tisk. "They're both soaked. I'm going to herd them closer to the fire before they catch their death of cold."

"I'll fetch some more hot cider," I said.

The longhouse had filled up while I had been out on the patio. A crowd of bodies, filling the space with a more humid heat than the fire managed, bodies that came with boisterous, loud voices and a plethora of elbows that seemed to thrust out of nowhere to catch me in the ribs as I made my way to the bar to fetch a tray and fill mug after mug with hot spiced cider.

I wasn't much use with magic on the fly, not yet. But I could catch hold of the protection spells that were already woven all around the mead hall and pull them closer around me as I hoisted that tray up on one shoulder and headed back through the crowd towards the patio.

Not that I was a novice with carting trays of food and drink around. But the diner I had worked at in my late teens and early twenties had never been as crowded as this mead hall.

Somehow, whether through magic or through the muscle memory of my time as a server, I made it back out to the patio without spilling a drop.

The others were standing around the bonfire now. Jessica and Gullveig were both shivering, but also grinning from ear to ear. Jessica was admiring Nilda's sword by the light of the fire, calling Michelle's attention to this detail or that as she examined the hilt and scabbard as well as the blade.

But as odd as that tableau struck me - did she really think Nilda had put that level of work into a Halloween costume? - it was nothing compared to the other side of the bonfire. Gullveig was holding her hands out to the flames, but she was also looking at the man next to her as he spoke with her.

I wasn't sure what was stranger, the fact that she was chatting with

Roarr, who nearly always kept to himself, or the fact that he appeared to be explaining s'mores to her.

"I'm sure it's all perfectly innocent," Loke said, appearing suddenly just over my shoulder. "It's just about the chocolate, really."

"What are you talking about?" I asked. "And where did you go just now?"

"I was here," he said with a vague gesture that might have meant the patio area, or all of Runde, depending. "And I was just putting your mind at ease. You were staring at Roarr like you were debating taking him down with a running tackle."

"I was not," I said. "Actually, what I was thinking is that he looks in very fine spirits. He's interacting with others and almost looks happy. Granted, I didn't know him before his fiancée died, but that's got to be a good change, right?"

"I suppose," Loke said as if he found the question boring. "Time goes on and all that."

"You *are* in a mood," I said. "Is something wrong?"

"Nothing at all," he said, with too bright of a smile.

"Are you sure?" I asked.

"I'm sorry. Am I bringing your party down?"

"No," I said. But then I looked back at the others gathered around the bonfire. "No, you're not bringing anyone down. But you are the only one who's not enjoying themselves this evening. Is there anything I can do?"

"Don't trouble yourself about it, Ingy," he said. "Everyone has low days. It's not necessarily a *problem* that has to be *solved*."

I knew the look on my face had to be deeply skeptical, or at least he sensed my intent to continue trying to draw him out, because something changed in his eyes. The warm brown became something flinty, and then he was giving me a sidelong look again.

"But I can see what you're enjoying here. It's like both your worlds are here at once, reflecting each other."

"What do you mean?" I asked.

"Don't you see?" he asked, taking the tray out of my hands and setting it aside on the picnic table before turning me back to face the others at the bonfire. He leaned close behind me to whisper in my ear. "You have two lives, two worlds, and everything that exists in one has a reflection in the other. Look, there's Michelle and Jessica, your closest friends in Runde. But in Villmark, it's Nilda and Kara."

"They don't look like mirror images," I said.

"I wasn't talking about looks," he said. "I'm talking about their roles in your life."

"Well, there's Andrew," I said, pointing to where he was standing next to Roarr. They were both chatting eagerly with Gullveig. "I suppose his mirror image is you, then?"

"Ingy, you disappoint me," he said. "Loke and Luke reflect each other. And trust me, you don't want to see another version of me out in the world. No, Andrew is your Runde Thorbjorn."

"He is not," I said. But mostly I was just suddenly sad. I never saw Thorbjorn enough. His responsibilities had him away from Villmark more than he was there, and his trips down the hill to the mead hall were rarer even than that.

"He is," Loke said confidently. "What I wonder is, when is that going to be a problem? Having two of them? I suppose if they never meet..."

"You're just stirring up trouble," I said, turning to face him. "You told me once you didn't do that, unlike your namesake. I believed you when you said it. Was I wrong?"

"I'm not stirring up trouble," he said, but he wouldn't meet my eyes.

"You're upset about something," I said.

"It's nothing. Really," he said, putting one hand over his heart and the other up in the air as if swearing an oath. Then he dropped his hands and spoke in a more normal tone. "My sister hasn't been well. Nothing serious," he quickly added, "but when she's down, I'm down. That's why I haven't taken you to see her yet. I'd rather wait for a better day."

"Of course," I said.

"You should hand out those ciders before they get cold," he said, reaching for the tray of drinks and handing it back to me. Then he stepped backwards, off the patio and into the darkness. He raised a single hand in a melancholy farewell before I lost sight of him entirely.

I looked down at the mugs on the tray. They were still steaming, if just barely. But it was as if Loke's down mood had been contagious, and I had been infected. I took a deep breath and put a smile back on my face before turning to head towards the bonfire.

Nilda, Kara, Jessica and Michelle gathered around me, fairly lunging for the warm mugs of cider. Andrew had moved closer to Gullveig, and whatever he was saying to her, she was listening to intently. I could scarcely blame him for not noticing my arrival. Gullveig was like a black hole of attention; she pulled it all into herself without really trying to.

Roarr was still caught in that gravitational pull himself, although much like Loke had just done, he appeared to have taken a step back from the warmth of the fire and was in the process of fading into the shadows that closed in all around the patio.

But his eyes were still on Gullveig. The opening up he had been doing just moments before was over now; he was once more quiet and reclusive, there but not engaging with the people around him. But the look in his eyes as he watched Gullveig listening to Andrew, that was new.

Inscrutable, but new. I worried about what it meant.

CHAPTER 3

It was midmorning about a week later, and I was sitting in the dried remains of my grandmother's herb garden. My cat Mjolner was stalking something, moving with slow deliberation, setting down one silent paw before picking up the other, his green eyes intent on something I couldn't see. Maybe it was something in his imagination, but if you told me my cat was hunting extradimensional beings that my mortal mind couldn't perceive, I wouldn't exactly disbelieve you.

I sketched him as quickly as I could in the frozen moments between his steps. The angle of his ears as he listened, the glint of the little hammer that hung from his collar as it caught the morning light.

Then finally he pounced into what was a little hedgerow of bristly thyme in the summer months. His tail whipped back and forth excitedly, and then he pounced again, deeper into the back of the garden and out of sight.

I looked down at the last sketch, little more than a scrawling of charcoal that just suggested a cat butt-up in a hedge. Then I flipped back, looking at my earlier sketches.

They might have all technically been depictions of Mjolner on his hunt, but as was usual for me, my hand without my knowledge had

CATE MARTIN

traced in a lot of extra details in the background. Not details of the garden, but cross-hatches that suggested runes to my mind.

That pressure was still building. Still! It was almost painful against my eardrums now, but I had no idea when it was going to finally break. I hoped it would end up being anti-climatic, maybe just a gentle snow or something. But my fear that it would be something far greater was drowning out that hope.

I was startled by a loud bang and turned to see my grandmother coming down the back steps from the kitchen. She had her coffee in one hand and a rolled up buttered lefse in the other, but the look on her face wasn't one of someone who just thought they'd look out on the morning sun and the lake while enjoying their breakfast. She was waiting for something, waiting with a little worry line between her brows.

"What's going on?" I asked, closing up my sketchbook and putting the charcoal away in my bag. "Mormor?"

"Here he is," my grandmother said. She raised a hand to point, but then seemed startled to find she was holding a coffee mug.

"Who?" I asked. I got to my feet and climbed the steps to where she stood, following her gaze to see Andrew walking up the road towards our cabin. His head was down and his watchman's cap and wool coat were too typically Runde to be distinctive, but I knew his walk well. His gait didn't look hurried, but I knew from experience how much work it could be keeping up with the stride of those long legs.

He stopped at our garden gate and reached over it for the latch, but then saw us both standing there watching him. "Ingrid. Nora. You have to come. There's been an accident."

"What sort of accident?" my grandmother asked as she opened the door to the kitchen and reached inside for her sturdy boots.

"Michelle and Jessica found a body," he said. "It looks like it washed ashore. We already called the police, but Jessica is really upset."

"I understand," my grandmother said solemnly as she tied up her boots.

"Was it a fisherman?" I asked. "Someone local?" Someone Jessica knew personally, again?

20

"No. Well, I don't know if she's local or not," he admitted. "I've seen her at the meeting hall a few times. I even talked to her on Halloween. She had an unusual name. I think it was Swedish?"

My grandmother looked to me. "Gullveig," I said to her.

"Yes, that's it," Andrew said.

My grandmother reached inside the cabin again to grab her walking stick and then pulled the door shut, waving for me to go down the steps first. I hoisted my bag up higher on my shoulder, then went to join Andrew on the road. If he wondered why I was bringing art supplies to go look at a dead body, it didn't show on his face.

"Are you okay?" I asked.

"What? Yeah," he said distractedly, then started walking back the way he'd come. I fell into step beside him.

"You were talking with Gullveig on Halloween," I said. "It looked like you two were really hitting it off."

"What?" he said again. It was like everything I said took a minute to soak into his brain. "Oh, yeah. We talked for a minute or two, but I think she talked to every guy there for a minute or two. Wait, does that sound bad? I just meant she was pretty popular. Not to say she was playing the field or anything..." He broke off with a groan of frustration. "I'm not saying it right."

"I get you," I told him. "I knew Gullveig. Not well, but well enough to know her attention was highly sought after, and she went out of her way not to be stingy with it."

"That's it," he said with a grateful smile that still had a touch of sadness in it. "Trust you to find the kinder way of saying it."

"Do you remember who else she was talking to besides you?" I asked.

"Why?" he asked. "You haven't even seen her yet, and you already suspect foul play? The police haven't even gotten there to suss things out, but you're already on the case?"

"It was just a simple question," I said. But in fact, I had already been 'working the case,' hadn't I?

Did my brain just jump to the worst possible conclusions now?

And yet, I had seen Gullveig swimming the day we had taken the

CATE MARTIN

Viking ship out on Lake Superior. She had been a strong swimmer, with endless stamina and a complete disregard for the frigid waters. They said the best swimmers are the ones who drown, but wasn't that a cautionary tale about hubris? Gullveig knew all of her advantages, but she never took any of them for granted. She knew she was attractive, but she always made sure everyone around her felt seen too. Something like swimming she took a lot more seriously. I couldn't see her taking risks in the water, overestimating her abilities so badly.

But it was November. Why was she in the water at all?

"There they are," Andrew said, pointing to where Jessica and Michelle stood huddled together on the rocky shore. I couldn't see the body from the road, but I could tell where it was from the point on the ground they were both trying not to look at.

The police hadn't yet arrived. I hurried my pace, leaving even Andrew behind until I reached my two friends. Jessica's eyes were red and her face was puffed up, but she was no longer crying, although Michelle was holding her so tightly it was like she was afraid Jessica would fall apart if she loosened her grip for even a moment.

"It's Gullveig, right?" Michelle said to me. She was still keeping her attention away from the body on the ground, looking at me and then at Andrew and my grandmother still walking towards us, and then at Jessica huddled close beside her.

I turned to look at the body. I doubted very much she had been killed here. The twisting of her limbs among the rocks looked more like the lake itself had spit her up and left her here. She was on her back with her face turned towards the lake as if she longed to return. The blonde hair that sprawled around her like a tangle of weeds looked drained of color, like its golden yellow hue had left with her last breath, leaving a colorless husk behind.

I leaned closer to get a better look at her skull and heard Andrew suck in his breath.

"I'm not going to touch her, of course," I said. He was always so worried I'd ruin a crime scene. "I don't see any sign of an injury, though."

"She just drowned," he said. "It happens. More than it should."

"Yeah," I said, but mostly I was wondering why she was wearing jeans. Jeans, and what had probably started out as a stunningly gorgeous blouse designed to bring out the blue in her eyes.

But no shoes. Her feet were bare.

I didn't realize I had shifted the bag on my shoulder around to my front and was digging out my sketchbook until I heard Andrew suck in another breath.

"Ingrid," he said with a shake of his head. "No." He pointed with his eyes at Jessica, who was watching me with genuine horror on her face.

"Sorry," I said, pushing the bag away. "I just... But no."

There was no way to explain that my urge to sketch what I saw wasn't a morbid desire to capture the moment. That it could be a way for me to discover clues that no police officer was ever going to find.

"They'll take photographs when they get here," Andrew said, as if that had been my motivation, capturing the crime scene for posterity.

"Ingrid," Jessica said. "Do you think this was an accident?"

Now I felt every pair of eyes on me. Andrew was mentally telling me not to answer; I got that message loud and clear. Michelle was as eager as Jessica to hear my answer, if a little afraid of what I might say.

But my grandmother had a whole other kind of curiosity. Like this was another test, and she was waiting to see how I did.

"If it wasn't, the police will be able to tell us that soon enough," I said.

"It looks like she just drowned," Michelle said, and I suppose I should've just agreed with her. She clearly expected me to, for the sake of the shaking woman in her arms.

But I didn't think what the moment called for was "tell Jessica whatever she needs to hear to be okay with this." And if asked, I don't think Jessica would think so either.

"It does," I said. "But there might be a reason for that, one we can't see without touching the body or running forensic sorts of tests. Maybe she hit her head or something."

"Or someone hit it for her," Jessica said with a wild fierceness.

"Maybe," I said. I could hear car tires on the gravel road and knew without looking up that the police had arrived. They would take statements, take photographs, do the best they could.

But the complications would start pretty much right away, when they found no record for anyone by the name of Gullveig. She had no ID, and nothing about her would be in any kind of file.

"Jessica, why don't you come back to the cabin with Ingrid and me?" my grandmother asked, gently extricating her from Michelle's arms. "If they ask where we've gone-"

"I'll tell them," Andrew said. "Michelle and I should be witnesses enough for just finding a body, though."

"Let's hope so," my grandmother said. She led Jessica away, the two of them murmuring together too low for me to hear.

I lingered a moment, looking down at the body as if I wanted to sear the image in my brain. I had my phone in my pocket; if I wanted a photo of my own, I had the means to get one.

But Andrew was right. The police would take all the photographs that were needed. I wouldn't capture anything they weren't going to get dozens of times over from angles I couldn't reach without moving the body.

No, a photograph wasn't what I needed to record. I needed to sketch. The urge to plop down on the rocks and put pencil to paper was nearly overwhelming. If Andrew hadn't still been there, watching me with disapproval waiting just at bay, I doubt I would've resisted that urge.

But the police were coming out of their cars now, and even without Andrew there, I no longer had the opportunity to sketch out a scene and hunt it for clues.

I followed my grandmother and Jessica back up the road to the cabin, but I already had plans to make a quick exit from there. Once Jessica was settled and I could leave without being noticed, I was going to head straight up the hill to Villmark.

I didn't know everyone who might have spoken to Gullveig on Halloween, but I knew for sure whom I wanted to start with.

Roarr.

CHAPTER 4

*M*y grandmother and I did our best, but it was really Mjolner who comforted Jessica.

Jessica sipped sparingly at the tea I had brought her, and only took a single bite of one of my grandmother's butter cookies, but the moment Mjolner hopped up onto her lap and demanded her attention, her breathing finally stopped hitching and the wild look faded a little from her eyes.

I looked at my phone for the tenth time, but there was still no message from Andrew. Were the police still there, or had they collected what evidence they could and left already?

"Do you need to be somewhere?" Jessica asked dully. She hadn't seemed to look up from Mjolner, and yet she had seen me looking at the screen of my phone.

"No-" I started to say, but my grandmother cut me off.

"You did have that one thing you wanted to get done this morning," she said. "What time was that meeting?"

"I didn't set a specific time," I said. "I don't think he's going to be hard to find."

"Don't let me keep you," Jessica said. "I'm just going to wait here until Michelle is done. I want to talk to her again before I open the café."

"Are you sure?" I asked, feeling guilty that I was leaving, but also guilty that I wouldn't be more help even if I stayed.

"Absolutely," Jessica said. "I'm not doing great, but I'll feel better in a bit, I'm sure. But stop in later, okay?"

"I will," I promised. I exchanged a glance with my grandmother, who raised her chin toward the door as if encouraging me to get a move on.

I grabbed my walking stick and hoisted up my art bag again, then headed out the front door, following the road to the meeting hall and then the narrow path that wound around the meeting hall to the wilder countryside beyond.

Everything was gray and colorless, the gorgeous part of autumn long since gone, but no sign yet of winter. It was cold enough for the dry grass underfoot to snap like little icicles. Not that I could hear that over the growing roar of the waterfall.

I climbed the steep path up the side of the bluff, then took the tight turn that led to the cavern behind the waterfall. The air here was coldly humid and a fine mist from the falling water had coated my wool cap and the hair that the cap didn't cover, but I knew they would quickly dry when I reached the bonfire in the cave beyond.

"Which Thor is guarding?" I called out, just as my grandmother always did.

"It is I, Thoralv," a voice said, so close it made me jump. Then the youngest Thor stepped out of the shadows at the deep end of the cavern. So far as I knew, there was nothing back there. Had he just been lurking there to give me a scare?

"Hello, Thoralv," I said. "Are you on your own here?"

"At the moment," he said, tapping his hands on the hilts of the curved knives hanging from his belt. "Nothing is coming through here that I can't handle."

"No, I suppose not," I said. "How is Thorbjorn?"

"Well enough, I suppose, although the last time I saw him he was with you," Thoralv said. He gestured for me to follow him down the narrow cave to the deeper cavern that held the ancestral fire. "He and Thorulv are on patrol, pretty deep in the hills, but they haven't called for the rest of us so I'm sure they're both fine. If a bit cold."

"I'm sure that's true," I agreed. Then more hesitantly I asked, "I don't suppose you know which side of things Loke is on?"

"Loke?" Thoralv repeated, stroking his beardless chin as if trying to remember who that name belonged to. "No idea," he decided at last. "He passes between the two villages at his own whim, but seldom through this cave. I find it best not to dwell on his methods. Did you need someone's help with something?"

"I'll be all right," I said. "I know you're on duty."

"I am, but I can summon others," he said.

"No, no need," I said. "I'm just here to speak with Roarr. He's in Villmark right now, isn't he?"

"So far as I know," Thoralv said. "Is this volva business?"

"It might be," I said. "I just want to speak with him now, not official business, but that might change, depending on how he answers my questions."

"Do you want me to keep him from passing through the cave?" he asked, touching those knives again.

"You know what? I think that would be a good idea," I said. "But don't hurt him or anything. I don't know that he's done anything wrong."

"What do you suspect he's done, if I may ask?"

I sighed. Of course, the news wouldn't have traveled from Runde to Villmark yet. Not if neither Loke nor I had carried it across the barrier. "Gullveig is dead," I said. "It looks like she drowned."

"Gullveig, drowned?" he said, his eyes wide. "That doesn't seem possible. Not only is she a fine swimmer, she has too much sense to tempt the fates by being out on the lake so late in the year."

"She wasn't dressed for swimming," I said. "She might've been on a boat and somehow fallen overboard."

Thoralv scoffed at that idea.

"Yeah, I don't think so either," I said. "You didn't see anything suspicious last night, did you? Anyone heading down to the boats?"

"No, but I wasn't on duty until this morning," he said. "I can ask Thormund. He was here last night."

"Please do," I said, gripping my walking stick more tightly. "I'm going to go talk with Roarr now, but I'll check in with you again before I go back home."

"I'll be here," he said. "Are you sure you want to speak to Roarr alone?"

"I don't know that he's done anything wrong," I said, "and anyway his parents will be there, so I'm sure I'll be fine. But if I get a bad feeling, I'll call out."

He looked me over from the top of my wool beanie to the toes of my hiking boots, lingering the longest over the walking stick and my bag of art supplies. I knew I didn't look like a volva, not without my grandmother's feathered cape draped around me and her bronze wand in my hand. Still, I drew my shoulders back and looked right back at him.

"You'll be fine," he said, "but whenever you have need, all of us brothers will always come running at your slightest summons."

"I know," I said. "I appreciate it, and I won't abuse that privilege. I'll see you in a bit."

"Farewell," he said.

I climbed the natural staircase at the other end of the cave and emerged in the meadow above the waterfall. The entire lake was spread out before me for as far as my eyes could see, but the first glimpse of it triggered a painful pressure on both of my ears. It was so sudden and so severe that I stumbled despite the walking stick in my hand.

This felt like more than a change in barometric pressure. Something more than weather was building over the lake.

I knew that in my bones, but my brain was stubbornly still unsure. If it were true that something magical was brewing, why was I the only one sensing it? Why me and not my grandmother?

I put the lake behind me and followed the path through the now-naked birch trees to the village itself. It was just past lunchtime, but with the cold most people seemed to be indoors until I reached the crossroads. Then I could see people bustling through the marketplace, ducking in and out of shops or chatting together on the cobblestone streets.

But I pressed on ahead, continuing along the main east-west road past house after house until I reached the one that belonged to Roarr's family.

I knocked on the door, and someone answered almost instantly, as if they had been waiting for me to arrive. But it wasn't Roarr or his parents.

"Hello?" I said to the blonde young woman who was blushing furiously as she looked out at me. I thought I recognized her, although I had only met her once. Most Villmarkers were some shade of blonde with either blue or green eyes, but the way this one wore her hair in a loose bun with tendrils curling around her shoulders was familiar. That, and the long white apron over her blue dress, were bringing up a specific memory from another day on this same doorstep. "Sigvin, right?"

"No, that's my sister," she said, and blushed even more deeply. "We're twins. The difference is the freckle. Hers is on the right, but mine is on the left." She touched the little fleck of brown, more beauty mark than blemish, on her cheek as if to demonstrate. "I'm Nefja."

"Oh, I see," I said, and put out my hand. "Pleased to meet you, Nefja. I'm Ingrid."

"Torfusdottir, I know," she said. "We all know you, even if we haven't yet met you."

"I suppose that's true," I said. My grandmother was a person of some importance, that was part of it. But mostly it was my red hair. Besides me, only the Thors had red hair, and theirs was more strawberry blonde than my fiery color.

"I don't mean to be rude, but I was just leaving," Nefja said. "I only stopped by to drop off some bread. Honey rye."

"Oh, yes! I had some of your sister's the last time I was here," I said.

"It's a family recipe," she said. Then she gave me an apologetic smile as she gestured that she needed to get by me.

"Is Roarr in?" I asked, not sure of the protocol for going into the house when another guest had opened the door and then abandoned the whole building rather than walking me inside.

"Yes, you can go on in," she said. Then she looked around as if to scope out eavesdroppers before whispering to me, "he's a little down today. I tried to get him to eat something, but he wouldn't do it. Maybe you could get him to at least have some bread and butter?"

My stomach growled loudly at her words, letting me know that in all the commotion that morning I had never quite gotten around to breakfast. But I ignored it. "Why is he down? Do you know?"

"Sorry," she said, shaking her head. "He has good days and bad days, but I never know which it is until I try talking to him, and I never, ever know why. Maybe he'll talk to you?" Her blue eyes lit up with hope.

She certainly had a lot of expectations for my visit. I blamed my grandmother, who pretty much went door to door in Runde and Vill-mark both, caring for everyone in big ways and small. Myself, I wasn't even sure where to start. But I nodded with feigned confidence. "I'll certainly see what I can do."

She smiled at me one last time, then danced down the steps to the garden. I watched as she let herself out of the gate, then gave me one last wave before heading back up the street towards the center of the village.

"Roarr?" I called as I unlaced my boots and left them in the mudroom with my walking stick. My art bag I kept with me, bulky as it was. In fact, I found myself clutching it tightly as I stepped up into the hall then followed it towards the back of the house where I remembered the living room to be, with its floor-to-ceiling windows overlooking the southern end of Villmark spread across the hill below.

"Hello?" I called again, not liking how small and tremulous my voice sounded. Nefja must have just left Roarr. So where was he? Where were his parents?

"Anyone home?" I stepped down from the hallway into the living room, the southern light through the windows temporarily blinding me. I blinked until my eyes adjusted, then looked up towards the kitchen that overlooked the living room, but no one seemed to be up there.

I started to turn to try calling up the stairs to where I assumed the bedrooms to be, but instead collided with a wide chest, stumbling back as I avoided the hands that reached out to steady me.

"Stop it!" Roarr said, throwing up his arms as if to protect his head. Like he thought I was going to start hitting him.

"Roarr, it's me, Ingrid," I said.

"I know who you are," he said, but he still had his face turned away from me behind his raised arms.

"Do you know why I'm here?" I asked.

"No," he said. Just a little word, but his voice imbued it with such epic sadness it tore at my heart. Of course, it wasn't strange for him to have down days. He had only lost his fiancée a few months before, after knowing her for most of his lifetime. How unmoored would I feel if that had happened to me?

I took a moment to gentle my own tone, to release the white-knuckled grip on my bag and untense my body language. But it took time to calm myself, and before I could get those calmer words out, he said something else that had my blood running icy cold through my veins.

"I mean, unless it's about that murder."

CHAPTER 5

$\mathcal{H}$e just let those words drop like they were just nonsense small talk, nothing of import, and turned towards the kitchen. "Nefja said I should eat something. I'm going to do that. You can come in the kitchen with me if you want."

For a moment I was frozen in place, probably with my mouth hanging open, although I was so numb I couldn't really tell. Was he confessing? Before I had even accused him of anything?

But then I ran his words back through my mind. No, that hadn't been a confession. Not exactly. But how did he already know about Gullveig if he hadn't been involved?

And his mood was all over the place. That epic sadness had shifted to something like serene acceptance, like the fact that I was there to talk to him about the murder was exactly what he needed to snap out of his fugue and remember that he needed to eat.

The smell of honey rye bread darkening in a toaster snapped me out of my own paralysis, and I scurried up the steps to the kitchen. Roarr was taking a plate out of a cabinet. He held it out to me with a questioning raise of one eyebrow and I nodded.

Well, I had missed breakfast.

"I'll have coffee too in a jiffy," he said.

"Roarr, we need to talk about this," I said.

"I know," he said. His shoulders started to slump resignedly, but then he steeled his spine and turned his attention back to setting out butter and jam. "I'm sorry if I seem offhand about all this. It's just that I've been waiting for you for so long."

"You have," I said, thinking back on the events of the morning. The time I had spent with Jessica and my grandmother, the time before that on the lake shore, the time it took Andrew to come fetch us. And I had no idea how long Gullveig had lain there before Jessica and Michelle had stumbled across her. Maybe hours. Maybe she'd been there since the day before.

"I can tell every time you look at me that you have questions you want to ask me, but you never do," he said. The toaster popped, and he divided the slices between the two plates and loaded up more bread before bringing the plates to the table.

"What do you mean?" I asked.

"You know what I'm talking about," he said with a flash of annoyance.

"Roarr, I don't think I do," I said. "I've just now come here, not exactly straight from the body, but I certainly haven't seen you in the time between. It's only been an hour or so since I even knew there was a murder." I didn't add, but I was thinking, that when I had tried talking to him downstairs in the living room he had refused to even meet my eyes. So what questions had he thought he saw in *my* eyes without even looking at me?

He had a slice of buttered toast halfway to his mouth. It hovered there for a long moment before he set it back down on the plate. "Ingrid, what are you talking about?"

"Gullveig," I said. "What are you talking about?"

"Gullveig?" he repeated. "What happened to Gullveig?"

"She was murdered," I said. "Last night or this morning."

"Murdered," he said. For a moment he looked like he was going to slip back into that slack-faced fugue state he so often favored. But then he covered his face with his hands. His eyes had just started to glisten wetly before he hid them from my view.

"Roarr-" I started to say, but he cut me off.

"I was talking about *Lisa*," he said, his voice muffled by his hands. "I am always talking about Lisa."

"Oh," I said. "I see."

He had been waiting for me to talk to him about Lisa? For months now?

But before I could ask about that, he lowered his hands. His eyes were red-rimmed, but he had choked back the tears I knew would've spilled if I hadn't been there. "Why do you think I murdered Gullveig?" he asked.

"We found her on the lake shore," I said. "She was dressed in modern clothes but with no shoes. Not dressed for swimming."

"It's November," Roarr said. "Why would she be swimming?"

"Hence the suspicion of foul play," I said. "Even if she had fallen off a boat or a dock or something, why wasn't she wearing shoes? Outside in November?"

"Foul play," Roarr said with a nod. "But you didn't answer my question."

"Why I suspected you?" I said. He nodded again. "I saw you talking with her on Halloween."

Roarr huffed out a breath and turned his attention back to his toast. "Pretty much everyone spoke to her on Halloween. Your list of suspects is going to be quite long."

"Maybe," I conceded. "But you seemed particularly annoyed with her. Because she was talking with Andrew."

"Who's Andrew?" Roarr asked. He was still pushing the toast around on his plate but making no effort to eat it.

"A Runde man," I said. "A friend of mine."

"Oh, that guy who hangs around with Loke," Roarr said. "Why would I care if Gullveig talked to him? Like I said, she talks with everyone."

"You weren't feeling jealous, maybe?"

"Oh, I see," Roarr said. "You think I was smitten with Gullveig."

"You weren't?" I asked.

"No," he said darkly. "I don't think I will ever feel again what I felt for Lisa. I certainly don't expect to."

"But you were talking with Gullveig," I pressed. "More than talking. You lit up being near her. I could see it."

"You don't know what you're talking about," Roarr said and pushed away from the table. He turned his back on me to fuss with the coffee, even though clearly neither one of us was making much of a go at having breakfast.

"I'm not trying to explain your own emotional state to you or anything," I said. "I can't say what you were feeling in that moment or any other. I'm just telling you what I saw."

He didn't answer me, just poured out two mugs of coffee, then turned to set them on the table. He didn't sit back down, though. Instead, he folded his arms over his chest and loomed over me.

"It's not like I don't understand why I'll always be a prime suspect in everyone's mind," he said. "I know how things look to the others. They don't know what I went through. How could they? But you do, Ingrid. You do. You disappoint me."

"What are you talking about?" I asked, but then I realized that I knew. "Halldis' spell?"

"She didn't make you do anything," he said. "She just kept you frozen helpless in a chair. But you know if she wanted you to do something, she could've made you do it. Your body was no more than a puppet to her, one she could control. And there would've been nothing you could've done to stop it."

"I don't know that at all," I said. "You said before you weren't sure how much of what you did was her directing you and how much was just you, choosing to play along."

"I never murdered anyone," Roarr said.

"Accessory after the fact," I said. "That's what we call what you did in the rest of the world."

"You mean moving Lisa's body? I couldn't undo what she had done, so what difference did it make? Nothing I could've done would've mattered. And nothing I do now matters."

"That attitude just makes you sound even more like a suspect," I said. "Maybe even the culprit."

Roarr glowered down at me, and I was all too aware of how much larger he was than me. If he wanted to hurt me, he could. And even if I summoned all five Thors to my aid, they'd never reach this kitchen in time.

I reached for my toast and crunched into it then looked up at Roarr with as unbothered an air as I could muster while I chewed.

I don't think he noticed the way my hand shook.

Finally, he expelled a breath and slumped back down into his own chair. "I was here all night with my parents," he said. "They can swear to that. They've been extra watchful since... well."

"I'm sure," I said.

"I don't own a boat, nor do I have access to one," he went on as if he hadn't heard me. "I guess I can't prove I didn't steal one from the harbor behind the waterfall."

"The Thors are comparing notes as we speak," I said. "If anyone did go down to the boats last night, I'll know soon enough."

"Then you'll know I'm not lying about that either," he said. Then he took a bite of his own toast, a bite half the size of the entire slice. "What more do you need from me?"

"Do you want to explain more about Gullveig?" I asked. "You said I had it all wrong. So enlighten me."

He washed his toast down with a long swallow of coffee, then wiped at his beard. "Did you know Gullveig was close with Lisa?"

"No, I don't think I did," I said. "I didn't think Gullveig spent much time with anyone from Runde."

"Not lately. Not since Lisa died," Roarr said. "But before? That was a different story. She even went to Duluth a few times to spend the weekend with Lisa at her college campus. They went to parties and things together. I only went to see Lisa one time. It was all too much for me. Too much noise, too many people, too many ways to say something wrong or stupid.

"But Gullveig doesn't have that problem. She loves noise and people, and she never feels foolish because of anything she said or did. She just fits in everywhere, you know?"

"I do," I said.

"But after Lisa died, I think all the joy that Gullveig took in your world, it died with her," Roarr went on. "She withdrew. Even here in Villmark, she didn't get out much. Not for weeks and weeks."

"Like you," I guessed.

"Like me," he agreed. "I've tried going back to my old routines, but they never feel right. I was starting to think they never would again. But then Gullveig was there, hanging with people from Villmark and people from Runde all together, just like she always used to. And she was, if not exactly as happy as she used to be, at least taking steps back to that place."

I sensed he needed a moment to gather his thoughts, so I didn't speak. I really wanted more of that toasted honey rye, but the crunch would be too loud, so I made do with another sip of coffee.

"I saw her moving forward, and I thought maybe I could do it too," Roarr said, his eyes on a melted pool of butter congealing on his plate. "I guess that was why I looked all lit up or whatever you thought you saw. I honestly don't remember this fellow you said I was glowering at. Like I said, she talked with everyone that night, and I had absolutely nothing to feel jealous over since I'm not now nor never was attracted to her in that way. But my mood did change that night. Because I can't push Lisa into my past as easily as Gullveig seemed to."

"That's understandable," I said. "You had different relationships with her. Your grief won't follow the same paths."

I was working hard to be diplomatic, playing the high-stakes round of "what would my grandmother do?" But I kept trying to recall exactly what I had seen in his eyes that night. It had been more than a week ago. Was my memory fuzzy? Was I imposing things on it in retrospect, in light of Gullveig's murder?

Or was Roarr lying to me now? Telling me what he thought I needed to hear to get me off his trail?

Was he that good of an actor?

He sighed and rubbed at his forehead, and the red tinge to his eyes grew a little more intense. "I guess you really don't understand what I went through, do you? Halldis kept you trapped, and you fought against it every moment with everything you had."

"I did," I said.

"Yeah, it was different with me," he said. "It was less aggressive, but more insidious. She took my feelings and my thoughts and my deeper impulses, and she subtly redirected them. Slowly, over time. Like training a vine to follow a trellis. The vine just thinks it's growing towards the sun, like it wants to. But the gardener is really the one in control."

"I'm not sure how I feel about that," I said. "Like you said, her spell was different on me. I'm not sure I'll ever know what it felt like to go through what you went through."

"You don't believe me," he said, his tone carefully inflectionless.

"I don't disbelieve you," I said. "I just don't know."

"Do you believe I had nothing to do with Gullveig's death?" he asked.

"For now," I said as I got up from the table. "Do you know what would help? You say Gullveig was close to Lisa in both worlds. You might stumble across a lead I'd never find on my own. I'm not asking you to investigate if that's too much for you to handle. If you need to just stay in and take care of yourself, I totally understand. But if you do hear anything that might help, let me know."

"I will," he said, also getting up to walk me to the front door. I snatched up the last of my toast to eat on my way back to my grandmother's house. "But I should warn you. I haven't been getting out much of late. I doubt I'll be able to turn up anything useful, even if I go hunting for it. I've... lost a lot of friends."

"Just, whatever you can do," I said. I held the toast in my mouth as I tied my boots so I couldn't speak again until I was stepping out the door. But I turned back to look at Roarr one last time. "The intention to help is the important thing. If you really want people to see you differently after all that happened with Lisa, you need to get out and become a part of things again. You have a lot of work to do to mend those bridges."

"Sure," he said, but he sounded tired, like he was about to lapse back into that fugue state, which would help no one. Least of all himself.

"I'll check in with you later," I said, and he nodded.

There was nothing I could say to him. Not until I had real time to invest in a proper conversation. So I just gave him a little wave, crossed his garden patio and let myself out of his front gate.

CHAPTER 6

I had closed the gate behind me and had just decided to head back to the cave to wait for Thoralv and hear what Thormund had said.

But then I saw Mjolner perched on a fence post on the other side of the street. He had been grooming his ears, not even looking my way, but I was sure he had been waiting for me. Especially after he finished bathing with a vigorous shake of his paw, then hopped down from the fence to slink up the cobblestone road, back across town towards the meadow.

When it looked like he knew exactly where he was going, I'd found it was usually a good idea to follow him. I ran to catch up and walk beside him. He gave me the briefest of glances out of the corner of his eye, but otherwise walked on as if on his own little stroll.

We passed through the cave, the bonfire now banked down to a soft glow of embers. Thoralv was still with his brother, then, or tending to another of the endless tasks those brothers shared. Mjolner didn't stop or even look around, so I pressed on as well.

He didn't stop at my grandmother's house either. The windows on the sides of the house that faced the road were smaller than on the other two sides, but I could see someone moving around in the kitchen. Probably my grandmother, but the only reason she would still be there so late in the day was because Jessica was still there with her.

"I thought your job was being an emotional support kitty today?" I said to Mjolner. He ignored me. Or at least, he didn't turn his head. But there was an indignant stiffness to the way he was holding his tail, as if I had offended him.

"Don't be mad. You're very good at it. I suppose that's how you wrapped up early? Jessica was doing well enough for you to slip away?"

The very end of his tail gave a little twitch. He had deigned to forgive me for treating him like a lackey, there for the pleasure of the humans.

No, he was most certainly not that.

We continued to where the road made a bend, shifting from following the river to following the lake shore. It was well past noon now, not that I could tell through the steely gray skies. But it was a high, benign cloud cover. No sign of the storm that my bones were still achingly foretelling.

A yellow fluttering something caught my eye. Police tape. Mjolner was heading towards it at his own slow pace, but I quickened my steps and lengthened my stride, anxious to see what the police had left behind.

The deep treads of tire marks on the gravelly beach. About a million footprints, the ones closer to the lake half-filled with water. Lots of little numbered flags that marked the location of since-removed pieces of evidence. And an enclosure of yellow tape that had already been snapped in several places by the ever-present wind.

I could tell where I wasn't supposed to go: the exact spot where Gullveig had still been lying when I had left this place earlier. But there was nothing else to show she had ever been here. Someone walking by now would have no idea what had happened here.

But *had* anything happened here?

Technically, it was possible. She might have been walking along this beach, decided for some reason to get into the water, and then drowned and washed back ashore. For all I knew, one of the numbered flags might be marking the location of her abandoned shoes. The flags extended much further from the body than I would've expected, and I hadn't taken a very thorough look around.

But I didn't think so. She would've had to have had a very good reason to attempt swimming after dark in November, and I just couldn't see her having one. If she had been attacked, she would've fought back. She would've run away, towards the woods that grew close around the mouth of the river, or to any of the houses on the shore where the Runde fishermen lived, or even up the bluff towards the highway. I couldn't imagine a single thing that would've driven her out into the water, especially not without drawing attention.

Still, I wasn't sure.

After circling the enclosure twice and examining each of the flagged areas without finding a single sign of a clue, I went to sit on a large, flat rock beside Mjolner.

"Was there something in specific you wanted to show me?" I asked. He just stared without blinking out across the lake. I counted three freighters on the horizon, but no fishing boats or sailboats. I didn't know if that was strange or not. I mean, I could see how no one would want to sail in this weather. I imagined most of the sailboats on the shore were stored away somewhere for the winter.

But surely fishing was a year-round job?

I actually didn't know. Which was embarrassing. Living in a fishing town, I really ought to know.

I put my chin in my hand and looked over at Mjolner again. He moved a little closer to press his warmth against my thigh, but otherwise didn't acknowledge my unspoken question.

Then I looked past him, at the cordoned-off area.

I hadn't gotten a chance to draw it earlier, but I could always draw it now, from memory. I had soaked up all the details I could when I had had the chance. That visual memory, plus the background of rocks that were still there, I was confident I could sketch out something pretty close to what I had seen.

I took out my sketchpad and pencils then got to work. The wind picked up while I was drawing, repeatedly blowing tendrils of hair across my face that I had to tuck back behind my ears. I could feel its icy touch on my cheeks and earlobes, and I could feel my skin starting to glow pinkly in response.

Then I lost all bodily sensation entirely as well as all sense of time. When I sat back and blinked I found my page filled with pencil marks, the entire scene before me intricately drawn, but as I had seen it that morning.

I didn't know how long I had been at it, but the tip of my nose was decidedly cold. I blew into my hand and pressed it to the center of my face. As I waited for some small warmth to return I realized the side of my thigh was cold as well and looked down to see Mjolner had left.

Typical.

I blew into both my hands and then rubbed them over my cheeks as I examined my sketch. Technically, it was well done, if maybe a bit morbid.

But magically? I wasn't seeing anything in it. It was a just a drawing with nothing deeper to tell me.

I leaned in to look at the marks where I had cross-hatched the dark sky, but nothing in that mass of detail was jumping out at me like a rune waiting to be interpreted.

I had felt close to something while I had been drawing, but for whatever reason I had failed to get it down on paper.

I closed up my sketchbook and put it with my pencils back in my bag, then headed back up the road. Again, I didn't stop at my grandmother's house. Instead I carried on, past the meeting hall and up the steep bluff path to the cavern behind the waterfall.

No one answered my call to, "Which Thor is guarding?" After the third try, I pressed on into the cave beyond.

And found the bonfire once more in full roaring life.

Was that because of me? Or a sign that Thoralv had returned?

Perhaps he had, but was patrolling the deeper complex of caves where I had never gone. I moved one of the three-legged stools that sat against the cave wall closer to the fire. It only took a minute for its heat to warm my wind-burned cheeks. And after another minute, I was pulling off my hat and unzipping my jacket.

I took out my sketchbook again. Maybe I would see something more while sitting here, by the ancestral fire?

Nope. Even by the dancing light from the flames, it was just as mundane as before.

I turned to the next page and took out my pencils. It was ridiculously easy to get into the artistic flow in this cave; I knew that well from trying it in the past. And soon after the artistic flow I felt that other fugue state kick in, the one where the magic moved through me.

And the magic was moving through me, but it wasn't flowing the way it was supposed to, from the world at large focused through my mind and hand onto the paper. No, something was... catching at it?

I could pull myself back to the waking world with one hard blink, but in that moment I was more curious than afraid. What was going on? This was most definitely new.

I kept my focus on the drawing emerging under the tip of my pencil, but whatever the mental version of the corner of my eye was, I was observing the flow of magic with that.

Yes, something was catching, and pulling, and twisting. I didn't see as it was having any real effect on what I was doing, but only because it didn't seem to be strong enough. It was like I was pulling taffy and a little child kept catching at it. They could tear off bits, but the bulk of the taffy was still being worked in my hands, still slung and pulled, then slung again over the hook before me.

For just a moment I shifted the center of my focus from my drawing to whatever was catching at my magic, trying to follow it back to the source.

The interference stopped at once, and I felt something racing away from me. I tried to chase it, but this sort of thing was way outside of my magical experience. I ended up with only a hint of a familiar smell, quickly gone.

And then I was snapping my eyes open and sucking in an enormous breath as if I had just been deep underwater.

"Ingrid?" It was Thoralv, who had pulled a stool of his own closer to the fire.

"I'm all right," I told him, although the hand I tried to rest on his arm in a reassuring way missed him by a mile.

That smell. I had known that smell. It was intimately familiar, and yet I couldn't quite name it.

"Halldis," I said, too loudly. She generated familiar yet unnameable smells with her spells.

"What about her?" he asked.

"Is she in her cell? Still held powerless?" I asked.

"Yes, of course."

"Are you sure?" I asked.

"Did she just try to attack you?" he asked, shifting on the stool to rest a hand on the hilt of one of his knives. For all the good those would do him against a real sorceress.

"I don't think so," I said. "My grandmother says she can't reach me now. I sometimes think she's watching me? But my grandmother says that's just a trick of my mind, because of what she did to me before."

"Your grandmother is very wise," Thoralv said, his tone carefully neutral.

Too carefully neutral.

"She might be wrong?" I asked.

He looked at me, and I could see that something was on the tip of his tongue. But then he shifted his position again, and his eyes changed, and I knew what he said next wasn't what he had been thinking a moment before.

"I will speak to the council," he said. "I'm sure your grandmother is right that there is nothing to fear, but on the other hand, there's no reason not to allay your nervousness by checking the wards again."

"Thanks," I said.

"Did she ruin what you were doing?" he asked, looking from me to the sketchbook in my hands.

"I don't know," I admitted. I looked down at the drawing. I hadn't quite finished it, but that only meant a section of the sky had only roughly sketched in clouds, waiting for details I hadn't gone back to draw later.

Still, nothing jumped out at me. I didn't discern a single pattern anywhere in the lines that might be a rune.

I flipped back to my earlier drawing, remarkably similar. My memory hadn't altered the scene in the slightest.

But something was different. I flipped back and forth between the two drawings, then settled on the second drawing, leaning in to look at the linework that formed the horizon.

"Does that look like a boat to you?" I asked, hovering a fingertip over the paper. It was so faint I was worried my graphite-stained fingers would rub it into obscurity at the slightest touch.

"Maybe?" he said.

"Is it?" I asked, not sure myself. "Wait, it's two boats. Two boats so close together they are overlapping."

"Ah, I see it," he said and gave me a satisfied grin. I must've had something doubtful in my eyes - I *was* worried he was just humoring me - because he reached around my shoulder to hover his own fingertip over the page. "Look. This looks like the prow of one of your Runde boats, but this one behind it is one of ours. I see it very distinctly."

"I do too, now that you point it out," I said. It was like seeing the sailboat in one of those 3D geometrical patterns. It was invisible until all of a sudden it was clear as day.

"This is helpful to you?"

"Very," I said, packing away my things and getting up from the stool.

"And your trip to speak with Roarr? Was that also helpful?"

"Not with this case, but I feel like I need to think some things through and then talk with him again later. But that's going to be a bigger conversation than I have time for now," I said with a sigh. Figuring out who killed Gullveig was almost guaranteed to be easier than figuring out what Roarr was really thinking.

"I spoke with Thormund," he said, with the air of someone who was giving up on being asked.

"Oh, sorry," I said, my mind still half on the Roarr Problem. "Did he see anything at all last night?"

"He did not," Thoralv said with finality. "But he wanted me to clarify that he never counted the boats, and he only patrolled the harbor twice. He cannot swear that a Villmarker hadn't moved through that area when he was not physically there."

"Okay," I said, not sure how to parse that sentence.

"You understand there is a barrier that separates Villmark from the rest of the world," he said, tracing out a shape with his hands that I wasn't at all sure was accurate. "The eastern edge fades off into the deeper hills, as you well know. But the western edge, mere feet from where you and I now sit, is a more definite border. We brothers feel it," he said, pressing a hand against his abs, "when anything foreign crosses over. But save for those who are marked, we do not get an alarm from a Villmarker crossing in either direction."

"Who is marked?" I asked.

"Only those we keep below," he said.

"Not Roarr, then?"

"Not yet," he said.

I thanked him again and hurried out of the cave, back down to Runde. But it was like the chill in his voice when he spoke those last two words had settled in my bones, keeping my shivering long after I had left the cold spray from the falls behind.

Roarr wasn't wrong to feel like he was never going to regain his place in society. It was going to take more than a few friendly gestures to thaw that glacier of distrust, and that was just with normally sunnily dispositioned Thoralv. I had very little idea what the rest of Villmark thought of him, but I really ought to find out.

But after I solved Gullveig's murder.

CHAPTER 7

*I*t was mid afternoon when I came back down the path from the waterfall to the back of the meeting hall. By this hour my grandmother would surely be inside, setting up for the night ahead. But she spent more time tinkering with her mead in the cellar than the two of us did together to weave the spells.

Not that I had the first idea about how to turn honey into mead, or even what that cellar looked like. It was like my grandmother's bedroom, never explicitly forbidden, and yet not a place I felt like I was welcome just going into.

But my grandmother never went inside my room either. I guess everyone needed their privacy.

"Ingrid!"

I looked up out of what I belatedly realized had been a daze to find myself halfway across the gravel parking lot in front of the meeting hall, heading towards my grandmother's cabin. Then I saw Andrew waving to me from the front door of the hall. I turned around and quickened my steps to reach him.

"You all right?" he asked.

"Yes," I said, not sure why he was asking.

"I had to call your name three times before you even looked up," he said.

"Oh. I was thinking about some things," I said. "Let's get inside and shut the door. It's not exactly warm out here."

He pushed the door wider to let me squeeze past him. I could hear voices further in, but I had to stand blinking for several moments before my eyes adjusted to the relative gloom. Then I saw Michelle and Jessica perched on barstools with mugs of something steaming hot. My grandmother was behind the bar, putting the finishing touches on a charcuterie board.

"Are you hungry, dear?" she asked me.

"Starving," I said. That slice of toast had only reminded my stomach that food existed, and it was growling louder than ever.

"Any news?" I asked as I dropped my art bag to the floor and slid onto one of the other stools.

"Nothing so far," Andrew said as he sat down beside me. Then he made the mistake of reaching for a slice of summer sausage and got his knuckles firmly rapped by the side of the cheese knife in my grandmother's hand.

"Wait for it," she told him, and went back to arranging little pickles and olives.

"Tea?" Jessica asked, getting off her stool to reach for the pot my grandmother had left wrapped in a towel behind the bar.

"Please," I said. "How are you doing, Jess?"

"Better than this morning," she said. I supposed that might be true, but there was still so much tension in her face.

"The café has been closed all day?" I asked.

"It's still the off season," she said. "It'll be all right."

"She'll open in the morning," Michelle said. "I'll be sure of that."

Jessica didn't say anything, just handed me the cup of tea. Earl Grey, to judge from the smell.

"I'm glad you're all here. I wanted to talk to you about something," I said. They all looked at me with eager curiosity, but before I could go on we were interrupted by the door banging open. But not the front door, the back one.

"Hey," Loke said as he strolled in.

"Luke," Andrew said, and I saw relief wash over his face. "I've been trying to reach you all day. Did you get my message? Did you hear the news?"

"We heard," he said, and then Nilda and Kara appeared in the doorway behind him. They were carefully dressed in modern attire, stiffly new jeans and roll-neck sweaters under jackets much like mine that kept out the wind. Nilda pushed past Loke to reach me first, pulling me off my stool to give me a tight hug.

Not that I needed one. But I could feel in her embrace how much she did. I hugged her back.

Kara hugged Jessica and then Michelle, then gently pulled her sister away from me to take her place.

"I'm so sorry, you guys," I said. "I know how close you all were."

"It doesn't feel real," Nilda said. Michelle put an arm around her while Jessica went to fetch more cups for the tea.

Jessica had a look on her face of studious intent, but at the same time some of the tension was easing from around the corners of her mouth. Like it helped her, having something to do, even if it was something small.

"Help yourselves," my grandmother said as she set the wood board loaded with food on the bar.

"Wow, Nora," Michelle said. "So much food, it's like you knew the others were coming."

My grandmother smiled enigmatically, but when she spoke all she said was, "I'm going downstairs to check on a few things. Ingrid, you should make some more tea. That pot's nearly dry."

"I've got it," Jessica said. She shooed my grandmother out of the way, but didn't object to Kara joining her behind the bar to help her get out more cups and spoons.

I turned to Loke and caught him by the arm, drawing him apart from the others. "You heard the news from Andrew?" I asked.

"Originally," he said. "But the word's all over Villmark now."

"Just that she's dead?" I asked.

"That she's dead, and that you suspect murder," he said. Then that old gleam made a brief appearance in his eyes. "That you questioned Roarr."

"And cleared him," I said. "I had no real reason to suspect him in the first place."

"Sure you did," Loke said. "Out of anyone in Villmark, he's shown he's capable of working to hide a crime."

Which, as I recalled, was a bigger crime than actual murder among the Villmarkers. Killing someone in the heat of passion? Understandable to them, although there was a price to be paid. But hiding the body? That crossed a line.

"Well, I don't think he was involved with this one," I said.

"You have a lead?" he asked.

"Sort of," I admitted. "Nothing really helpful like a name or description of the perpetrator or anything."

"Well, we're here to help," he said.

"That's why Nilda and Kara are here? To help solve the crime?" I asked.

"Gullveig died on the wrong side of the waterfall," Loke said. "No one else in Villmark is going to come down here to investigate this, and no one on this side is even going to know who she is. We seemed uniquely qualified," he said. Then he summoned a grin, if a shadow of his usual one. "You're going to need the assistance of both of your teams."

"I think you're right," I said with a sigh. But then I added, "thank you."

He gave me a little bow, but again none of the usual merry light was in his eyes.

Something was so clearly bothering him. Why wouldn't he just talk to me about it?

Yeah, when I was done solving this crime, and had that long overdue talk with Roarr, I'd have to find a way to get Loke to open up a little. You know, in the time I wasn't already devoting to my magical studies and my actual job of creating art and trying to find buyers for it.

Always nice to have plenty of line items on my personal to-do list.

"Ingrid?" Andrew said, realizing I was no longer sitting next to him. He turned to see me and Loke standing apart from the group. Loke took half a step back to where he could safely disappear in the shadows. But I knew he would stay there, listening, even contributing if he felt he had to. I went back to the bar.

"Is there anything we can do to help?" Nilda asked me.

"Help with what?" Jessica asked eagerly. Now that the job of making tea was accomplished she was on the hunt for the next thing to do.

"There is," I said. "There is something I can use everyone's help with."

"What's that?" Andrew asked.

"Well, I've been asking around about last night," I said. "I don't know anything actually helpful, or I would bring it to the police, of course."

I said that for Andrew's benefit, of course. He was always worried I was going to ruin the official investigation of whatever. If only I could tell him that this was like Lisa's murder, not something the police could ever solve.

"What is it?" Jessica asked as she handed me a plate. She had selected a little bit of everything from the charcuterie board, and my stomach loudly reminded me that the toast from before was long gone and totally inadequate in any event. I munched on a few of the nuts just to get it quieted down, then turned to the others.

"I have a lead," I said. "Maybe."

"Where did you find a lead?" Andrew asked.

"It doesn't matter," I said, waving the question away.

His eyebrows shot up, and I knew he was about to argue the point when Loke offered, "anonymous source?"

"Yes, an anonymous source," I said, nodding. "And it's not solid, or again, I would've taken it to the police."

"All right," Andrew said, relenting. "How can we help?"

"There may have been fishing boats out on the water last night," I said. "Just two."

"Suspects?" Jessica asked.

CATE MARTIN

"Or witnesses," I said.

"Maybe one of each," Michelle said.

"Do you know anything about the boats?" Nilda asked.

"I know one was from Runde," I said. "And the other was from your hometown."

Now it was Nilda's turn to raise her eyebrows. Kara sat up straighter on her barstool, and I knew they both understood exactly what I was saying.

"How did your source recognize the boats?" Andrew asked. "How did they know where they hailed from? Were they on the shore or what?"

"I don't know," I said. "I didn't actually speak to them. I just got the message. Vague, right?"

"Not much to go on," Jessica agreed.

"It's a start," Nilda said, giving her arm a squeeze. "We can ask around our town, find out who might've been out on the water after sunset."

"We'll do the same here in Runde," Jessica said. "And I know just who to ask first."

"Sure," Michelle said as if reading her mind, "but there's also-"

"I know," Jessica interrupted her. "I have a list, actually." She tapped her forehead.

"Let's write that list down," Michelle said. "It'll be easier to see if we're both on the same page when it's actually, you know, down on a page."

"I'll help," Andrew said, grabbing a few more slices of summer sausage before joining them at one of the rickety tables.

"I reckon we know just where to start as well," Kara said, and Nilda nodded. Both of their faces were so grave, it made my heart ache.

"Are you sure you guys are up to this?" I asked. "This has to be painful."

"No," Nilda said. "Painful is what's going to happen to whoever did this."

"It's still possible it was an accident," I said.

54

"You don't believe that," Nilda said with total confidence.

"Do you?" Kara asked.

"I don't know," I admitted. "All I'm saying is, we're likely hunting down whoever was on these two boats to find witnesses. No one is a suspect until we know they did something suspicious."

"We won't hurt them," Nilda promised me. Then she and Kara sat down at one of the other tables to start their own list.

I walked over to where Loke was still lurking in the shadows. "Are you going to join them? Make the groups even?" I asked.

"You mean be your Villmark Andrew?" he asked me with a crooked grin.

"I thought Thorbjorn was my Villmark Andrew," I said, "and you were your own thing. Luke. Loke."

"I *am* my own thing," he agreed. "But do you need a Villmark Andrew?"

I couldn't tell if he was just winding me up or seriously asking me something. I knew if I ever needed Thorbjorn that I could call and he'd come running. But this didn't feel like the sort of situation that would require calling him away from whatever he was doing. Patrolling for giants? Hunting bears? Wrestling with the trolls again?

"No, one Andrew is enough," I said. "And I don't think there's anything going on here that needs Thorbjorn's skills."

"I'd have to agree with that assessment," Loke said. "So what do you need?"

"In a word?" I asked. "You. You move between the worlds more than anyone else I know. You belong in both places more than I do-"

"Not quite," he interrupted me with a single raised finger. "I will concede that I belong in equal measures to both places, but it is also true that I also don't belong to either place in equal measures."

I took a deep breath. "My point is," I said, "Gullveig was dressed like a modern woman when she died. I don't know what she was doing or with whom, but if anyone can help me figure all that out, to figure out what to make of whatever my separate teams bring back to me, it's you."

At first he just looked back at me without saying a word. But then slowly that familiar grin spread across his face. "It's good to have my unique set of skills appreciated," he said.

"I see you," I told him. "Even when you're hiding in the shadows. Now, come on. We have work to do."

CHAPTER 8

There really wasn't anything I could do to help that night. Michelle, Jessica and Andrew knew people in Runde I had never even met, and the same was true of Nilda and Kara in Villmark. Not only did they know their names, but they had enough of a nodding acquaintance with them to not freak anyone out if they asked the first, most basic questions about where they were and what they were doing.

Not to mention I was needed at the meeting hall, to help my grandmother transform it into the mead hall. She could do it without me, of course, but when I weighed what use I would be in the first narrowing down of their respective lists versus how much I still had to learn about using and controlling magic from my grandmother, I really only had one choice.

So I sent my teams out to canvas their respective hometowns while I remained behind to assist my grandmother.

At some point, Loke had just disappeared. Whether he had other leads to followup on his own or just his own affairs to attend to, I had no idea. But I knew he'd turn up when needed for the next phase of the investigation, so I didn't worry.

It was a quiet evening in the mead hall, and an even quieter night curled up in my bed in its attic nook, Mjolner purring away on my pillow with his spine pressed against the back of my neck.

I had agreed to meet the Runde team at Jessica's café before she opened. That meant getting up early and taking a long, cold walk, but at least there'd be fresh coffee and pastries at the end of it.

The air was indeed quite cold when I stepped outside, and I snugged my wool cap a little lower over my ears and made sure the cuffs of my jackets covered the end of my gloves so my wrists weren't exposed. I was still getting by with my fall windbreaker and hoodie combo, but I could feel parka weather coming not too far in the future.

I had the strap of my art bag slung across my body, but I left my walking stick behind. I had enough time to take the longer way to the café, the one that followed the road along the lake shore around the curve of the bluff then took the path up the less steep side of the bluff to the highway above. I went that way more to see the lake than the crime scene.

The sun was low over the water, a dark red circle that didn't seem to be radiating any heat at all, just concentrating it within itself without sharing. It looked so small and so far away. I wondered if that was how the sun looked from Mars or even Saturn.

That sense of impending change was still pressing against my eardrums. I took my phone out of my pocket and looked at my weather app, but nothing was on the forecast except more of the same gray but rainless days, daytime temperatures flirting just above freezing.

As I was putting the phone back in my pocket, I noticed I had a companion. Mjolner was walking with me, or rather a few paces behind me. He was looking out over the water again, as if he hadn't noticed me there either.

"Mjolner," I said, and he gave me a brief glance. "Heading up to the café?" I asked him. "I know Jessica loves it when you hang out with her there. Not that I don't still think she shouldn't get her own cat. I bet you'd like the company, right?"

Mjolner gave me a slow blink then looked out over the water again.

"I know," I said to him. "It's full of fish. Must be maddening for you that it's so cold and so wet."

He ignored me.

We climbed the path up the bluff to emerge behind the café. A truck barreled past on the highway, stirring up a gust of wind that whipped at the ends of my jacket.

I opened the door and a blast of warm cinnamon-scented air washed over me. So much nicer than the oily smell of the truck wind. Mjolner slinked past me to head for his favorite puffy chair and I pulled the door shut behind me.

"Now we're all here," Andrew said from where he was sitting with Michelle at one of the tables in the reading area between the bookshop and the café. Michelle turned in her chair to give me a smile. She was already dressed for work, a cardigan over her server uniform and her honey blonde hair in its high ponytail.

"Coffee?" I asked as I tugged off my gloves.

"Help yourself from the pot," Jessica said as she emerged from the back room with a pan full of steaming cinnamon rolls in her mitted hands. "Unless you want an espresso?"

"No, coffee is fine," I said, letting her pass to set the pan on the table before heading behind her counter to the coffee machine. "Any news?" I asked as I took a mug down from the shelf over the machine.

No one was saying anything, but when I looked back over my shoulder, they were all beaming at each other, so I guessed the quiet was just because there was a deadlock over who was going to speak first.

"Jessica, you were the one who put his name on the list," Michelle said. "You tell." She tried taking a roll, but they were still too hot, so she contented herself with licking icing off her fingertips.

"Andrew was the one who noticed he was at the party on Halloween," Jessica said. "That was what put him over from witness to potential suspect."

"Wait, what's going on?" I asked as I carried my coffee back to the table. "Someone start at the beginning."

"Well, we had the list we showed you last night," Jessica said.

"A lot of names," I said, nodding.

"Yeah, but I guess we shouldn't have been surprised when nearly everyone we spoke to said they never went out yesterday," Jessica said.

"The day before yesterday," Andrew corrected her.

"Yeah, the day before yesterday now," Jessica said. "The water was getting choppy, so most called an early night."

"Which maybe you knew? Since you said there were only two boats out," Michelle said to me.

"I didn't know that specifically, but you're right. We shouldn't be surprised," I said. "But you did find someone who was out?"

"Just one," Jessica said.

"Although we contacted everyone on the list," Michelle added, in case I thought they had found one and stopped.

"You talked to him?" I asked.

"Not yet," Jessica said.

"He wasn't in when we called, but his mother told us he was definitely out alone on his boat," Michelle said. "And then Andrew..." but she trailed off, letting Andrew pick up the thread while she made a second, more successful lunge at the cinnamon rolls.

"Then I remembered that I had seen him at the meeting hall for the Halloween party," Andrew said.

"So he might have known Gullveig," I said.

"Oh, they met," Andrew said almost smugly. "They most definitely met."

"What?" I asked. "Did something happen?"

"He was flirting with her," Jessica said. "She was polite. I mean, Michelle and I could see how she was just being polite."

"More polite than I would've been," Michelle grumbled.

"He was aggressive?" I asked.

"Well, more like persistent," Andrew said, and the other two nodded their agreement with that assessment.

"Interesting," I said, and Jessica beamed.

Of course every man there had flirted with Gullveig to some extent during the course of the night, and maybe even some of the women. But I didn't speak that thought out loud. Jessica clearly thought it was an important clue. I didn't want to burst her bubble. Not when it might not even be a bubble.

"I should go talk to him," I said.

"You mean *we* should go talk to him," Michelle said.

"You need us," Jessica said. "We're locals."

"I mean, you're local too, now, but-" Michelle started to say.

"No, I get it," I said. "You're right."

Jessica was practically dancing with excitement. "We should go now, before he goes out for the day."

"But what about your café?" I asked. "You were closed all day yesterday. Do you really want to risk being closed two days in a row? I mean, you should really be selling these cinnamon rolls rather than feeding them to us for free."

"It's been slow lately," Jessica said, but I could see she was torn. She loved her business. More than that, she knew how much work she needed to put in to it for it to thrive. She couldn't take it casually or it would fail.

And yet, she so clearly wanted to be there when I spoke to our potential suspect. Who might end up just being a witness, but that could be exciting too.

No, that wasn't fair to Jessica. It wasn't excitement she was looking for. She wanted justice, and she wanted to help get it.

"Andrew," I said, turning to face him. "Are you doing anything today?"

"No," he said, drawing the word out a tad. I suspected he wasn't being entirely truthful. But he pressed on. "I'd be happy to help in any way I can. Provided we go to the police the minute we know anything solid."

"Of course we will," I said. But then gently added, "so, can you watch the café for Jessica? It should only take us an hour or so."

"Can you, Andrew?" Jessica asked eagerly. "You know all the prices, and you're the one who showed me how to run the register in the first place."

"And you can run the espresso machine too," Michelle said. He looked doubtful, but then she said, "it works just like the one in the restaurant. You remember."

"Oh, yeah," he agreed. "Sure." He gave us all a smile, but it wasn't a smile that lingered long on his lips.

He had been my investigating buddy on the last case, even driving to other towns with me to chase down clues. I knew he thought that would be the case again this time, and although he didn't say it out loud, I knew he was hurt that I was sidelining him.

"Can we walk to this place from here?" I asked Michelle and Jessica.

"Yeah, it's not far," Jessica said. "We'll go grab our coats. Andrew, you're sure you're up for this?"

"Totally," he said to her, flashing that temporary smile again. She gave him two thumbs up then ran to the back room to get her coat. Michelle was already taking hers down from the rack near the door, hunting through the pockets for her hat and gloves.

"Thanks for this," I said to Andrew. "You can see how much it means to Jessica."

He brightened at that, and I realized he had been worried I was deliberately excluding him for some unknown reason. "Yes, I can see that."

"This could help her find closure, or a sense of peace, about Lisa," I said.

"Maybe," he said, but then leaned closer. The two of us had already been speaking in low tones, but now he dropped to a whisper. "Just make sure you're safe. Anything feels off at all, just back away and call the cops."

"Of course," I said.

"Promise me," he said, putting a hand on mine.

"I promise," I said. "I'm sure we're just going to talk to a witness and not a murderer, but I'll be on my guard. Promise."

He took a moment, but in the end he nodded his acceptance and took his hand off mine.

Then he turned to Mjolner, who rather than sleeping all curled up on his favorite chair was sitting upright like he had been a member of our little meeting. "Do you hear that, Mjolner?" Andrew asked, and the cat blinked in reply. "It's just you and me, boy. We man-types are holding down the fort while the women go solve the murders. But we've got this. We will not let them down."

Mjolner winked one eye at Andrew. But then he looked at me, and I felt like his eyes were explicitly reminding me of what I had just promised Andrew.

Although the rescue he was imagining if we got in over our heads was probably less a police one and something more cat-based.

"We'll be fine," I told him, then went to join Michelle and Jessica at the door.

"Text if you need me," Andrew said.

"The same goes for you," Jessica said. Then the three of us were out the door and back down the path towards the lake shore.

CHAPTER 9

$\mathcal{W}$e scrambled down the steep path until it met the
lakeside road. Then Jessica and Michelle turned to the
left to continue following the road to the north. I had walked this way
a few times before while I was just out wandering on my own. It was
all residential, the houses set far from the road, more a walk in the
woods than anything.

The strip of land between rocky bluff and the shore was narrower
here, but the trees were thicker. The aspens and birch had lost their
foliage, but the evergreens that dominated were full and tall, blocking
any possible line of sight up to the highway. I could occasionally catch
a glimpse of the lake, but only little snatches. Most of the homes were
out of sight, only their driveways and mailboxes giving them away.

"There's my house," Michelle said, turning to give me a grin as she
pointed to the left. I could see the mailbox with "The Larsens" spelled
out in reflective letters along with the house number, but when I
looked up the driveway I saw it appeared like it was heading straight
towards the rocky bluff only to take a sudden righthand turn and
disappear in a thick stand of evergreen trees.

"I can't quite see it," I said.

"It's tiny," Michelle said with a little shrug. "No lake view or anything, too shady for a garden, and we're practically right under the highway. But it's perfect for my mom and I."

"It's just the two of you?" I asked.

"Since my brother moved to Michigan," she said.

I wondered why she didn't say anything about a father, but I decided if she wanted me to know she would've mentioned it herself. Instead I asked, "So this guy we're going to talk to is a neighbor of yours?"

"Simon?" Michelle said with a frown.

"Is that his name?" I asked.

"Simon Eklund," Jessica said. "And I guess technically he's been our neighbor since forever."

"He was two years ahead of us in school," Michelle told me. "I guess we rode the school bus together, but I don't remember him ever saying two words to me."

"He was in Andrew's grade, but they hung with different groups," Jessica said. "Andrew recognized the name when I mentioned it to him this morning, but not much else."

"So he still lives with his parents?" I asked.

"He fishes on his dad's boat. They work together," Michelle said. "He's still single, so I guess he doesn't need his own space yet."

"There's not really a thriving housing market in Runde," Jessica said. "Most of us still live with our elders."

"Hey, I'm not judging," I said, holding up my hands in surrender. "I lived with my mom until she passed, and then I moved right in with my grandma. Apartments are expensive, and my friends who do live with roommates and not family are largely miserable."

"Andrew has his own place," Michelle said. There was a conspiratorial gleam to her eye when she looked over at me that made my cheeks flush. Why was she telling me this?

"Sort of," Jessica said.

"It's his own place," Michelle insisted. "It's just a cabin, and it's on his grandfather's property, but he doesn't share a wall let alone a kitchen or living room with any of his elders. But what am I talking about? Surely you've already been there."

"I haven't," I confessed with what I hoped was a casual shrug. "I keep pretty busy, you know. Most of the time when I see Andrew, I'm seeing the two of you as well. At the meeting hall."

"Or the café," Jessica added.

"You could change that in a heartbeat," Michelle said.

"What, being busy all the time? I don't think so," I said.

"You know what I mean," Michelle said, and that gleam was back in her eye. Clearly Loke wasn't the only one who liked to stir up a little mischief.

"Here it is," Jessica said suddenly, to my immense relief. "The Eklunds. We talked to his mother last night and told her we'd be stopping by. She said she'd tried to keep him from leaving, but no promises."

"No one is going out today," Michelle said with a grim certainty.

"Really?" I asked, trying to peer through the trees to take a look at the sky over the lake, but it was still hidden from view. "Because of the weather?"

"The weather?" Michelle frowned. "No, this is nice for November. No, the news has gotten around about Gullveig. Her body being found, I mean. That spread too late yesterday to keep the boats ashore, but today I'm sure everyone will be taking a day off in her memory."

"People are freaked out," Jessica whispered to me, as if the trees that closed tunnel-like around the narrow driveway were trying to eavesdrop. "Everyone thought she was a local, but now that she's dead, no one knows who her people are."

"Did *you* think she was local?" I asked.

"I thought she lived south of the river," Michelle said. "I don't know why. I just pictured her doing farm chores."

"Gullveig?" I said, but she just shrugged. I couldn't imagine Gullveig doing farm chores. Riding a winged horse and fetching the souls of the battle-dead, sure. But farm chores?

"I thought she was from the north end of town," Jessica said. "I swear I even thought I knew which old guy was her widower dad. I mean, my imagination filled in all the details. But the police say she has no ID, and there is no record of anyone by that name anywhere near here."

"That's weird," I said, making a mental note to grill my grandmother again about how the spells worked. Was this part of what she did to protect her mead hall? That was certainly where everyone from Runde who knew Gullveig had met her.

Or was it part of the older magic, the spells that hid Villmark from the world? I had seen the effects of how they worked in real-time, blasting away at the short-term memory of the police officer who had attempted to question me on my first day in Runde. He must have asked my grandmother who she was five times. Were fake memories another version of that same spell effect?

Of course, there was always the possibility that Jessica was right about her imagination. Sometimes the mundane answer was the right one, after all.

At last we found ourselves climbing the steps to the front porch of a little house that looked in danger of being swallowed up by the trees crowded around it. The paint was of a particular shade of green that had last been fashionable in the seventies, but the canopy above had protected it from the sun well enough so that it was only peeling in a few random spots.

Michelle took the lead, swinging open the screen door to knock on the front door. After a moment, she rose up on tiptoe to peer in the diamond-shaped window set in the door. She dropped back down at once. "She's coming."

The door opened, and a short woman appeared. She looked dressed for the weather with a thick sweater over a flannel shirt over a thermal undershirt, but then I saw her bare feet were thrust into a pair of faded pink bedroom slippers.

"Hello, Mrs. Eklund," Michelle said cheerily.

"Michelle," she said, and Michelle nodded enthusiastically. "Yes, I thought I recognized you. It's been a while since we've had a night out, but it was at your restaurant. My husband had steak and potatoes, of course, but I had your fish of the day. Haddock, I believe, but served with the most divine creamy lemony sauce."

"My mother's proprietary sauce," Michelle said. "I only pray she leaves me the recipe in her will because she won't tell me a thing about it now."

"Hmm," Mrs. Eklund said, nodding repeatedly even as she sounded like she'd lost the conversation's thread already.

"Mrs. Eklund, we called last night?" Jessica said. "We wanted to talk to your son Simon?"

"Simon," she said, then looked each of us over in turn. For some reason, I felt like I was being evaluated as potential girlfriend material. That impression didn't fade when she turned her attention back to Jessica before saying, "he's in the back, dear. In the fish-house. If you follow that path there, it will take you right to it. If you hit the lake you've gone too far."

Jessica laughed at her little joke, ignoring Michelle's raised eyebrow.

"Thank you for your help," I said.

"Hmm," Mrs. Eklund said. Then she smiled at Jessica. "I hope to see you again soon, dear."

"Well, I run the new café up on the highway," Jessica said, not catching Mrs. Eklund's actual meaning at all, I thought. "We have books and art and lots of baked goods. You should stop in some time."

"Perhaps I will," Mrs. Eklund said with another smile. Then she stepped back inside her house and pulled the door closed behind her.

"Matchmaker, matchmaker," Michelle sang to herself as she skipped down the steps. "Shall we?"

We followed the path, really just a bare patch in the already sparse lawn. Behind the house, the trees finally spaced out to give us a view of the lake. A boathouse sat right on the water, another smaller building beside it. The path was heading straight towards both of those.

"Have you ever been in a fish house?" Jessica asked me as we reached the smaller building.

"I can't say that I have," I said.

"They aren't cleaning a catch today," Michelle said with a chastising look directed at Jessica. "It'll be fine."

Oh. Jessica was warning me about the smell. I could imagine it pretty well. Jessica wasn't the only one with a detail-supplying imagination.

But as it turned out, Michelle was right. When we stepped inside the gloomy interior, we found it too dark to see until we gave our eyes time to adjust, but luckily, even if our other senses were made stronger by the lack of visual information, the smell was tolerable. Fishy, to be sure, but not freshly fishy.

"Who's there?" a man's voice asked.

"Didn't your mother tell you we wanted to talk to you?" Michelle asked, blinking as she tried to find the source of the voice.

Then there was a rustle of motion and we all found him at the same time. He had been sitting under a window, completely obscured in the shadow, especially with what appeared to be a football field's worth of fishnet strewn all around him. He had blended in with the wall, and it took him a moment to get it all off his lap so he could step out of it and walk towards us.

Like his mother, he was on the short side, and he had a swagger to his walk, like someone who desperately wanted to project taller. His eyes were narrowed as he approached us, but then a spark of recognition flashed in his eyes and he tipped his head and nodded at us with a smile that pulled up to one side.

"Ah. The Giggle Twins," he said.

"The who now?" I asked, looking from a furiously blushing Jessica to an equally red Michelle.

"That was our nickname," Jessica hissed at me in a whisper.

"In grade school," Michelle said out loud and crossed her arms over her chest to glare at Simon. "I can't speak for Jessica, but I haven't *giggled* in decades."

"But why twins? You don't even look alike," I said, still confused.

"Because they're both Larsens?" Simon said, raising his eyebrows in an overly incredulous look.

"But no relation," Jessica said.

"Well..." Michelle drawled.

"Well, maybe generations back," Jessica said. "But half the town is either Larsens or Swansons. That twin thing was always kind of stupid."

"Whatever," Simon said with a shrug. "My mother said you called, but that's all the information I have on that matter. Does anyone want to explain? Because I have work to get back to."

"We wanted to talk to you about Gullveig," I said.

"Who?" he asked. I didn't answer, just watched as the furrow of his brow smoothed out and he said, "oh, her. The mystery woman found washed up on the shore."

Jessica started to bristle up beside me, but she calmed when I placed a hand on her arm. "That's all you remember her from?" I asked.

"Should I know her from something else?" he asked. "Unlike these two, I never rode a school bus with her. Believe me, I would've remembered that."

"What about from Halloween?" Michelle asked. "Would you remember her from that?"

He frowned again, then started worrying a thumbnail between his teeth. He really seemed to be trying to remember. Trying, and failing. I didn't think he was acting. I glanced at Jessica and she looked worried, like her big lead was about to be a bust. So I guessed she thought he was being sincere too.

Only Michelle continued to glare at him like a teacher waiting for a better excuse than "the dog ate my homework."

"She was wearing a valkyrie costume," she said to him as a prompt, but his frown only deepened.

"I think half the women there were dressed as valkyries. I must've missed a movie or something," he said.

"She was the one who looked like a supermodel," she said. This time his eyes widened.

"I *do* remember her," he said. "Yeah, she was gorgeous. Crazy gorgeous."

"He remembers," Michelle said, throwing up her hands.

"I remember her being there," Simon said. "Lots of people were there. Are you tracking everyone down who was at that party?"

71

"We will if we have to," Jessica told him, and he looked startled by her aggressive tone. I supposed if his mental image of her was stuck in grade school, her current demeanor would be jarring.

"Wait, you think I had something to do with this?" he asked, putting a finger over his own heart. "That party was more than a week ago. I haven't seen her since."

"I imagine it would be hard to prove that," Jessica said.

"Yeah, it would," he shot back, getting annoyed. "Not that I have to. You're not the police, and even if you were, I don't have to prove I'm innocent. You have nothing on me, no reason to suspect me." Then he scoffed, shaking his head as if unable to believe what was happening. "Because we were at the same party? Come on."

"Actually, that's not why we're here," I said. "I wanted to ask you about the night before last."

"The night she died, I'm guessing," he said, clearly still irritated.

I nodded. "There were two boats out on the water after sunset, when we think whatever happened happened. One of those boats was yours."

"Yeah, I was out late that night," he said. "I had trouble with one of the nets. Well," he said, sweeping a hand to where he had been sitting under the window, clearly mending a net when we came in.

Jessica's face darkened, and I could see just what she was thinking. Some dark image of Gullveig tangled up in a net, weighted down underwater, trapped until she drowned.

Only, there hadn't been any marks on her. If she had struggled against that net, it would've left marks. Rope burns. Something.

So I put my hand on her arm again in a silent signal, and she again held her tongue, although this time she shot me a quick look, as if urging me to get at the truth. Quickly.

"Were you out alone?" I asked.

"Probing my alibi, are we?" he asked, looking at each of us in turn. "Again, not that I have to explain myself to you, but I was. Completely alone. No girl on the boat with me. My father was with me in the boathouse when I went out and when I came back in again if you want to ask him."

"We will," Jessica said, despite my hand still on her arm. She gave me an apologetic look, but there was still angry color in her cheeks.

Well, Simon's attitude was grating on me as well.

"We don't need an alibi," I said. "The police might ask you for one, but like you said, no one has any reason to suspect you."

"So, what?" he asked, raising his empty hands palms-up.

"I don't think you're a suspect," I said, trying for a trusting smile. I don't think what I managed was particularly convincing. At least it was dark in the fish house, so I had that going for me.

"Great," he said and rolled his eyes.

"We just wanted to ask if you saw anything," Michelle said. She had dropped her crossed arms and stepped forward with a pleading look. "Anything at all. You were out there when she..." She broke off, taking a moment to get her quavering voice back under control.

Simon's growing annoyance vanished in a flash. If anything, he looked a little freaked out that she might start crying right there in his fish house. His hands reached for her, then fell away again, unsure of what he should do.

I had to admit I was impressed. I had to sneak a glance at Jessica to be sure that Michelle was faking. The slight upturn of the corner of Jessica's mouth was the only hint I was right.

"Sorry," Michelle said, wiping at her eyes with the back of her hand, then giving Simon a trembling smile. "Sorry. She was a friend."

"Yeah," Simon said, plunging his hands into his pockets. "Yeah, and you guys were close to Lisa too, right?"

"We were," Michelle said. "And the police never solved that one. We're really worried this one is going to slip away too."

"Sure," he said, nodding. "Sure."

"*Did* you see anything?" I asked.

He chewed at his lip for a moment. "You said there was another boat out there?"

"We think so," I said. "We haven't found who might've been out on it yet, though. Did you see another boat?"

"Like a fishing boat? No," he said. "Not after sunset."

I nodded. This was what I had expected. The other boat had been a

Villmarker boat. It could've been sitting in the water right next to him and he never would've noticed it. They all had protective spells on them, old ones. They worked even without my grandmother on board. She juiced them back up once a year, but I hadn't seen that spellwork yet.

"There was a yacht, though," he said.

"A yacht? In Runde?" Jessica asked.

"Yeah, right," Simon laughed at the image, then grew serious again. "No, not really near Runde. It was way out there, practically over the horizon. I could only see it because it was all lit up. I remember wondering who would want to be out on a party boat in November, but I guess if you have a boat like that you have money to burn trying to heat up the great outdoors."

"So you didn't catch a name, then?" I asked.

"No, sorry," he said, shaking his head. "But I doubt it means anything. That far out? They didn't see anything. And even if your friend had been on that boat and was... if she fell overboard or something, the water would've carried her miles away from here. She wouldn't have washed up here, no way."

"Okay," I said, pulling my sketchpad out of my bag and tearing a corner off a blank page. "This is my cell number. If you think of anything else, will you call me?"

"Sure," he said, shoving the paper into his pocket without so much as glancing at it first.

"You can also find me pretty much anytime at the meeting hall," I said.

"Oh, sure. Nora Torfa is your grandma," he said, nodding as if relieved to have that mystery solved. "I knew I'd place you eventually."

The three of us walked in silence back up the driveway until we reached the road.

"Do you think maybe that yacht was the other boat your informant mentioned?" Jessica asked, but before I could answer I felt the cellphone in my pocket start buzzing with missed texts.

Ah, Runde, with your patchwork of cellphone coverage, more patch than work. Never change.

As I scrolled through the texts, I realized both Jessica and Michelle were waiting for me to answer the question. "No," I said, tucking the phone back away. "No, the two boats spotted were both fishing boats. But maybe the other fisherman saw this yacht too."

"How will you know?" Jessica asked.

"I'm about to go talk to him right now," I said, patting the phone in my pocket. "That was Luke. He's with Nilda and Kara. They have a name."

"Well, get running," Michelle said, giving me a playful shove up the road that was hard enough to send me stumbling. She didn't know her own strength.

I gave them a little wave, then jogged down the road as fast as my heavy, bouncing art bag would allow.

And felt an immense gratitude that neither Michelle nor Jessica had asked me why I thought it was that Simon had never mentioned seeing another fishing boat at all.

CHAPTER 10

$\mathcal{J}$ found Nilda and Kara waiting for me in the front garden of their house, sitting on benches around the cheery flames of the fire pit. But I could tell at a glance that finding their quarry had not brought them the same satisfaction that it had to Jessica and Michelle.

"Is it bad news?" I asked as I held my gloved hands out to the flames. The wind had been brisk across the meadow over the waterfall. Although the walk to the village had kept most of my body warm, my hands despite the gloves and my cheeks appreciated the fire.

"He's not going to want to talk with us," Kara said. "It's going to be tricky."

"Luckily for you, I'm good with tricky," Loke said as he emerged through the gate. Despite his jocular words, he looked if anything even more down than the sisters.

I took a deep breath. It was time to pull my team together. "Who is the suspect or potential witness or whatever?" I asked.

"His name is Raggi," Nilda said.

"A fisherman?" I guessed.

"He is," she said. "He usually goes out in one of the larger boats with several of his friends to fish together, but I gather on the evening in question he was alone."

"Well, if we're clear when we talk to him that we are treating him as a witness and not a suspect, what's the problem?" I asked. "I mean, if he seems suspicious, that might get thorny, but that's not the feeling I'm getting from the rest of you. You're acting like just talking to him is going to be difficult."

"It will be," Kara said. "He's a strict isolationist."

"Okay, you're going to have to explain that one," I said.

"It's just what it sounds like," Loke said. "He leaves the boundaries of Villmark to fish because that's what our ancestors have done since Torfa brought us here centuries ago, but he never mixes with outsiders."

"So he's not going to like talking with me?" I guessed.

"Or me," Loke said with a half-hearted grin.

"Or us," Nilda added. "Everyone knows we go down to your grandmother's mead hall regularly."

"He won't talk to you because of that?" I asked. "But that's... When my grandmother works the magic on that hall every sunset, she extends the Villmark protection to include that building."

"Your grandmother is the first volva to have ever done that particular magic," Loke told me. "It was never done before. Mixing with the outsiders like that?" He gave a mock-sorrowful shake of his head.

"Only it *was* done before," Nilda said, staring fixedly into the flames as she spoke. "Even in Torfa's day, we traded with the local Ojibwe. A village can't sustain itself without outside trade. Our ancestors would've starved."

"Not to mention the frightening inbreeding," Loke said with a shiver.

"But just trying telling Raggi and his ilk any of that," Kara said. "They won't hear it. Not even if you show them their family's entries in the Book of the Settlement."

I could hear in her voice that those words were capitalized. "What's that?" I asked.

"A record of everyone who came over with Torfa from our ancestral island home in Norway," Loke said. "It records their names and family connections from back home, then continues down through every descendant to modern times."

"It must be huge," I said.

Loke shrugged. "When people move away, they disappear from the book. And we gain new people without importing more than their own name and origin, not their entire genealogy."

"People have always gone off on their own, or married outside our people, or brought someone from outside in to marry," Kara said. "Not many. Not the majority. But enough."

"Or, as I said, the inbreeding," Loke said.

"Okay," I said, setting a thousand questions aside, starting with a request to see that book. "So Raggi isn't going to want to talk to me or Loke, and will be irritated having to talk to either of you. Is that the gist of it?" I asked.

"That's the gist of it," Nilda agreed.

"If only Thorbjorn were here," Kara said wistfully. "He can talk to anyone."

"I don't want to call on him unless there's no other way," I said. "Let's just try talking to him ourselves, and if we really get nothing..." I trailed off, throwing up my hands. I really didn't want to get in the habit of pulling Thorbjorn away from his own work whenever I ran into an obstacle. "Do we know where to find him?"

"No one went out on the water today," Kara said. "We already checked. That means he will be with his buddies at the mead hall they favor on the west of town."

"They are all staying in because of Gullveig?" I asked.

"Well, they'll claim some augury about changing weather, but yeah. It's about Gullveig," Kara said.

"It's a shame she's not here," Nilda said. "She's another one who can talk to anyone."

We walked up to the crossroads, then turned left to follow that road past Roarr's house to the very edge of the village.

This was further than I had ever gone in this direction. I had walked beyond the village to the north, into the deep forest and hills that would've gradually become the mountains of Norway if I had kept going. The furthest south I had been was the public gardens, but nearly every house I had been inside of sported a southern view, down the slope of the hill to a valley of fields where Villmark grew its food and kept its animals. And of course to the east was Runde and the lake.

But the west was something different. There were rolling hills of trees now bare of leaves. I supposed it could have been the Superior National Forest I was looking at, but I suspected that parts of it were, like the land to the north, not quite what basic cartography would seem to dictate. Like if I kept walking in that direction I wouldn't go back to Norway like in the north, but I wouldn't be in Minnesota anymore either. Maybe I'd go on to some strange new land.

Thorbjorn would know what lay beyond those hills, but I wasn't sure he would tell me even if I asked.

"Here it is," Kara said, pointing out an unassuming structure half-built into a hillside. The roof that jutted out from the hill was A-frame, but covered in sod now as dry and gray as the rest of the November world around us. There were no windows, and around the closed door the wood frame and stone walls were stained with what looked like the smoke of generations.

"It looks old," I said.

"It's not the oldest place in Villmark," Nilda said. "But there are only two older. The council hall and of course the caves below."

"Shall we?" Loke said, reaching past the three of us to pull the door open.

Like in Simon's fish house earlier, I found myself having to step into a dark gloomy space and wait for my eyes to adjust. Although Kara had called it a mead hall, it was beer I smelled. That and smoke and grilled meat. The meat smell was the strongest and freshest of all, and I could hear the hiss as juices from that meat dripped onto the fire.

Then Loke let the door fall shut behind him, and with that light gone my eyes started to pick out details. Without windows, the only light was from the fire pit that dominated the center of the room. Half of that was banked to glowing embers to slow-roast the meat, but the other half had been built up into bright flames. It did an adequate job of lighting the space when the door was closed, but it also made the room uncomfortably warm and I immediately unzipped my jacket.

Which was probably a mistake. At that little whisper of noise every head in the place turned to stare, and I realized that we would find Raggi here because this was where all the Villmark isolationists felt most at home. And I had just announced myself as absolutely not one of them.

"Sorry," I said, although whether to my friends or the strangers around us, I couldn't say. I pulled the wool cap from my head and stuffed it with my gloves into my pockets.

"We're looking for Raggi?" Nilda said.

"Who's we, then?" someone asked. I looked around but couldn't tell which of the faces still turned our way had spoken. They were all sitting at tables with their hoods up, their faces in shadow, like everyone was here for some more clandestine purpose than beer and a light lunch.

"It's Ingrid Torfudottir," a woman said as she emerged from the shadows at the back of the room. She was wearing a liberally stained apron and was carrying a pair of tongs that looked like they dated back to the Viking Age.

"I am," I agreed. "May I ask your name?"

"Aldís," she said as she used the tongs to turn the meat on their spits.

"Is Raggi here?" I asked.

"He's just over there," she said, nodding her head back over her shoulder as she leaned over the fire. "And he'll hear you out if he knows what's good for him. A volva recognized by the council still means something in my establishment, and any who wish to be welcome here would do well to remember that."

There was a low murmur around the room, and most of the customers turned back to their own beers, bowls of stew, and plates of dark bread. But one man who was sitting at a back table with three others raised his arm. "I'm here," he said. "Raggi."

"Raggi," I said, looking nervously to each of my friends before crossing the room to stand before his table. I drew myself up tall and did my best to remember every correction Nilda and Kara had ever made to my pronunciation of the variant of Norse spoken in Villmark. "Well met." I looked from Raggi to the others at the table, but they were all ignoring me, their hooded heads bent low over their food. I turned my gaze back to Raggi.

"Well met," he returned grudgingly. But then he got straight to the point. "What business does a volva have with me?"

I swallowed hard. Unlike nearly everyone else in Villmark, he wasn't going to generously switch to English for my benefit. This was going to be tough. I had been letting my language lessons take a back seat to my magic lessons, and it was about to show.

"You were out on the lake the night before last?" I asked haltingly.

"I was," he said, turning his attention back to the bowl of stew I had interrupted.

"In my vision, I saw one of the smaller boats. But I understand you usually go out with a group. Is this true?" At least with this interview, I didn't have to hide my sources.

"Yes, you saw true," he said after chewing a mouthful of what looked like elk. Even the more rarely cooked interior was darker than beef or bison, and there was very little fat. "The boat needed repairs. I left the others to tend to that while I went out alone to try to salvage something of the day."

"And you were out past sunset?" I asked.

"Well past," he said, but then added again, "alone."

"Did you see anything while you were out on the water?" I asked.

"What am I meant to have seen?" he asked, sucking juice from his fingers, but at least he was setting the food aside to give his full attention to me.

"I'm guessing if you'd seen Gullveig you'd just say so," I said.

"I wouldn't have even waited for you to ask," he said. "I would've killed any man out there who set a hand on her if I saw it."

I supposed it was just as well he never came down to my grandmother's mead hall, then.

"Any other boats?" I asked.

"There was a fisherman out, also alone, I thought," he said, still sucking at his thumb. "From Runde." He said the name with the modern pronunciation, thoroughly wrong to his ears, and his disdain of it came through clearly.

"Yes, Runde. Runde," I agreed, saying it both ways. The U in the correct pronunciation was a bit tricky, like a German umlaut, but a bit more whispery. I thought I nailed it okay, but Raggi's face remained as impassive as ever. "Anything..." I broke off, rolling my hand over and over as if I could churn up the word I didn't know.

"Suspicious," Loke finished for me.

"Suspicious. Anything suspicious?" I asked, grateful for the assist. Raggi looked past me, his eyes narrowing and his mouth curling down as he glared at Loke. "Raggi?"

He looked back at me. "You think this Runde fellow did this?" he asked, and his hands on the tabletop twitched as if about to form fists.

"No, I've already spoken to him," I said. "Unless you saw something-?"

"No, he did nothing that I saw," Raggi said, then smirked. "Except fail to catch a sizable school of fish that swam right into my nets, nice as anything."

"Lucky for you," I said. He shot me a dark look, and I belatedly realized that clearly he thought this was a matter of his superior skill and was just being humble about it. "Did you see anything else? Anything nearby?"

"Another boat, you mean?" he asked, watching carefully to see how I reacted to his question. I nodded. "Yes, there was one. I'm guessing you know of it already."

"I do, but I confess I do not know how you would describe such a boat in your language," I said.

He looked at me consideringly for a long moment, as if weighing annoyance at my lack of knowledge with a grudging respect for not trying to cover that lack up.

Then a buzz sounded. Not loud, but jarring as every conversation around us died out at once. I knew that sound. It was a cellphone set to vibrate. I felt my face flush as I patted my pockets, but it hadn't been mine.

"Sorry," Loke said, pulling out his own phone to look at the screen. It was like he had brought something rankly evil into a holy place to judge by the horror-filled looks on all the faces around us. Then he looked up, saw everyone staring at him, and mustered up a grin. "I'm going to take this outside?"

"Yes, please," I said, not sure why he was asking my permission.

"Good to see you," he said to Raggi, then nodded at each of the others at the table even though they were still studiously ignoring us. There was a flash of blinding brightness as he went back out into the noonday world. Then the door clanked shut and the fire-lit darkness returned.

"They call it a yacht," Kara said to break the silence. "We don't have a word for it. But you know of what she speaks."

"I do," Raggi admitted. "It was far off, at the very horizon where the truly large ships pass by. But this wasn't one of those. This was smaller, all lit up as if desperate for all to see it from miles away."

"Did you see any markings on this ship?" I asked. "Sometimes there is a name painted on the side, or maybe a number?"

"It was too far," he said, shaking his head. "And even if it had not been, I do not read your letters."

"You're trying to find out what happened to Gullveig?" Aldís asked, wiping her hands on her apron as she came over to the back corner where we stood.

"I am," I said. "I'm not having much luck so far, but I'm far from giving up."

"That's good that you're looking into it," Aldís said. "I loved that girl. We all did."

"You knew her well?" I asked.

Aldís gave a tearful smile. "She spent many an evening here. I know she went down the hill to your grandmother's hall on occasion, but most nights she was here."

"As well she should be," Raggi said.

"Well," Aldís said, clearly striving to be diplomatic and not speak ill of my grandmother to my face. But at the same time, she glowed with pride at his words.

"Has she been here since Halloween?" I asked. I had lapsed into English with that last word out of necessity, and she looked at me with unfeigned confusion. "Um, in the last week or so?"

"Oh, yes," she said. "Like I said, she's here most nights. In fact-" she said, but then something passed over her face, and I could see her change her mind over what she had been about to say. Instead, she repeated herself. "Yes, most nights."

"You were going to say something else," I said. She shook her head, taking half a step back. In the next second she was going to plead some chore that required her immediate attention, and I reached out to touch her arm and make a more personal plea, when Raggi spoke again.

"It's all right, Aldís. I have nothing to hide," he said, and relief washed over Aldís' entire body.

"What are you not hiding?" I asked.

"I proposed to Gullveig," he said. "Right here in this very hall. Twice. The second time was just three nights ago, so within the time you are asking about."

"Twice?" I said.

"She turned me down," he said. "Twice."

Motive. He had a motive.

That thought must have shown on my face, because Raggi gave me a dark look. "I wanted to marry her. She was the best of us, but she was slipping away. I wanted to convince her to commit to our culture and our ways."

"I understand," I said, reaching for the same diplomatic tone that Aldís had deployed so well, but judging by Raggi's sneer, I had not hit my mark.

"Do you?" he asked. "Do you understand that I offered her everything I had, I laid it all at my feet, and when she dismissed it, I regathered my courage and offered it to her again?"

"And she turned you down again," I said, still aiming for a neutral, nonaccusatory tone.

"And I was prepared to regather myself yet again," he said, his voice nearly a growl. His friends still did not look up at us, but I could feel a lot of bodies around us tensing up, preparing for action if action should be warranted.

"I do," I said.

"Do you?" he spat back. "Or are you just thinking that's all you need to hear to decide I was the one who killed her?"

"I haven't accused you," I said, curling my hands into fists as I fought the urge to take a step back. Brightness flashed across the room again as someone came in or went out the door behind me, but I didn't dare turn away to see who. "I won't accuse you. Not without..." Words failed me again.

"Proof," Kara said for me. "She, like her grandmother, will judge all fairly. Including you. You may rely on that."

"I'll decide what I rely on," Raggi said. "But hear this. If any should accuse me of murder, I shall take that accusation as a question of honor. And I shall respond to that accordingly."

I opened my mouth to ask what that meant, but strong hands grasped my arms and started pulling me back towards the door.

"We understand," Loke said, and I relaxed when I realized it was him pulling me away. "And, hey! Thanks for your time!"

I didn't see how Raggi reacted to that last remark because the door was once more open and the room and everyone in it disappeared under a cover of too-bright light. And then I was back outside.

CHAPTER 11

"*Y*ou hustled us out of there in a hurry," Kara said. To my immense relief, in English.

"Raggi was getting heated up, but nothing we couldn't handle," Nilda said. "We had Ingrid's back."

"Yeah, thanks," I said. I felt a little shaky. Although I hadn't been afraid in the moment, now that I was out of that hall it was like my brain was letting in all the stimulus it had blocked out. Those people in there had not liked me in their place. If Raggi had gotten any more angry, things could've gotten ugly in a hurry.

"In future, if you need to come back here for any reason, bring a Thor," Loke said. I could see in his eyes that he was absolutely not joking, and that made my hands shake even more.

"I will," I promised. Then I said, "who was on the phone?"

"Wait, that wasn't a ruse?" Nilda asked.

"No, it was Andrew," Loke said. "There is no one in Runde with a family connection to Gullveig, but in the last few weeks he's gotten friendly with some of the police officers who keep getting dragged into town."

"They told him something? Something important?" I asked.

Loke nodded then took a deep breath. "There was a date rape drug found in her system when they did the autopsy. Her blood alcohol was barely elevated, like if she'd had a few sips of wine or something, but a lot of this drug. A lot."

"Like whoever did it didn't know what they were doing?" I asked.

"Or were trying to be very sure?" Loke ventured. "If they knew Gullveig at all, considering her stamina..."

He didn't finish his thought, but I shuddered anyway. "They didn't know what kind?"

"He didn't say, but does it matter?" Loke asked.

"Maybe. Maybe not," I said.

"It rules out Raggi, anyway," Loke said. "No way he would use something so modern when clubbing her over the head would work just fine."

"That's a bit crude," I said. Nilda and Kara were looking back and forth between us as we spoke. I got the sense that "date rape drug" was a new one for them, but since it pretty much explained itself, they had no questions, just the same revulsion Loke and I were sharing.

"I don't think he's a suspect," I said. "For that reason, but also I believe he is just the sort of guy who would keep proposing no matter how many times she said no. But not hurt her."

"No, that would lack honor," Loke said.

"So, what now?" Kara asked. "Is there anything else to follow up on? That yacht, maybe?"

"There doesn't seem to have been anyone else on the water," I said with a sigh. "Simon and Raggi's stories are very much the same. Nothing out there but that yacht, and no sign of Gullveig."

"Maybe she was on the shore when she was drugged and tried to get into the water to get away when she realized what was happening?" Nilda said.

"Where would she hope to go?" Loke asked.

"Away," Nilda said with a sad shrug.

"Well, we've chased down every witness on the water. I guess the shore is all that's left," I said.

"But you didn't draw that," Kara said.

"Maybe because I didn't specifically try to," I said. I tried to remember what I had been picturing before I had started sketching. Both times, even before I had set pencil to paper, I had been focused on the lake. But did that mean anything? "I've been trying to figure out some feelings I've been getting from the lake for weeks now," I admitted. "It might have muddied my process. I'm still new at this."

"Well, we can ask around again," Nilda said. "More general questions. By this point, with everyone talking about it all over the village, if anyone saw anything, it will be pretty easy to chase them down."

"That's probably as good a plan as any," I said. "Thanks, you two."

"Find us if you need us," she said, giving me a quick hug.

"And good job on the Norse," Kara said as she too hugged me. "Your pronunciation is getting really close."

"Thanks," I said, and waved as they walked back towards the center of town.

Not that Loke and I had any other direction to go. But we took it more at a stroll.

"Off to the cave, then?" Loke asked. "Have another stab at a drawing?"

"It doesn't feel like that will help," I said. "Maybe I should go back to where Jessica and Michelle found her, or walk up and down the shore from there."

Then I looked up and saw Mjolner once more sitting on the fence post opposite Roarr's house. But he wasn't waiting for me, or at least he wasn't looking my way. He was watching something moving back and forth in front of him, and I followed his gaze to see a woman in a blue dress and snowy white cloak pacing in front of Roarr's garden gate.

Loke beside me stiffened and was about to take flight, but I put a hand on his arm. "It's not Sigvin. It's Nefja." Not that I knew why he always ran away when Sigvin approached. It was just another one of his little eccentricities.

"You're right," he said, and relaxed, but only a little.

"I think she has a thing for Roarr," I said.

"Her and half the women of the village," he said with a disapproving tisk of his tongue.

Then Nefja heard us approaching and turned, apron balled up in her fists under her cloak as if she had been wringing it in anxiety. She released it almost like she was throwing it to the ground, then ran forward to meet us, catching both of my hands and giving them a painful squeeze.

"Oh, good! You're here!" she said.

"I am," I said. "What's going on?"

"I came here to meet Roarr," she said. "We were going to have lunch together." She made a vague gesture behind her and I saw she had left an overly full basket by the gatepost. It was covered in a thick homespun cloth, but I had to imagine there was enough food under it to feed a family of six.

"Okay," I said. "Did he ditch you?"

"Ditch me?" she repeated as if the words meant nothing to her. But she just shook her head and plowed on with her story. "His mother says he's not here. That he left this morning, early. Very early. To watch the boats come and go."

"Is that strange?" I asked, glancing from Nefja to Loke, who just shrugged. "Doesn't that just mean he's up on the meadow?"

"That's what his mother thinks he means, but it's not," Nefja said. Her cheeks, already colored from the cold air and her furious pacing, flushed a brighter pink at the idea that she knew just a touch more about Roarr than his own mother did.

"What does it mean?" I asked.

"No one is even out today," Loke said. "Every boat in Villmark and in Runde stayed ashore."

"That's true," I said, then looked questioningly at Nefja.

"He goes further away to watch boats," Nefja said. "He says it calms him. Boats come and go, but the harbor remains."

"Which harbor?" I asked. There was no harbor in Runde. There was a harbor of sorts behind the waterfall, but somehow I doubted that was where Roarr liked to go to be alone. And there weren't many boats there to watch either.

Then another thought struck me. I turned to Loke. "Is it possible he knew about the yacht?" I asked. "Simon and Raggi both saw it.

Simon doesn't go to the mead hall often, although he was there on Halloween. It took a bit for him to even remember it when I was talking to him; I doubt he's told others. Especially if Roarr left early this morning."

"You're asking me if Raggi would've told Roarr?" Loke asked, and I nodded. He stroked his chin as he thought this over. "Normally, I'd say no. But Nilda and Kara weren't quiet about their investigation. If Roarr knew they were looking for a fisherman who might've seen something, he could've gotten Raggi's name and gotten to him first."

"Wouldn't Raggi have mentioned it when we talked to him? That he'd already had the same conversation with Roarr?" I asked. Loke shrugged.

"Do you want me to go back and ask?"

"No," I said. "It doesn't matter. I'm just thinking-"

"That he's looking for a specific boat, and not some calming exercise," Loke interrupted. "Yeah, I'm thinking the same thing."

"If he left Villmark, Thoralv would've seen him pass," I said.

"Maybe," Loke said. "There are, after all, other ways in and out. And we know for a fact that Roarr knows at least one of them."

"That's true," I said with a sigh. "But when I talked to him yesterday, he really did seem like he was trying to regain people's trust. Being sneaky wouldn't do that."

"It's cute how you think people never lie to you," Loke said.

"Nefja," I said, pointedly ignoring Loke. "Do you have any idea where this harbor is? Anything he told you?"

"No," Nefja said. "Just that it's not in Villmark. I know that because it's a secret. He doesn't want his parents to know. They worry."

"Okay," I said. "Nefja, can you do me a favor?"

"Anything," she said eagerly.

"Can you stay here and watch for Roarr? And get word to me when he comes back?"

"Certainly. But how do I reach you?"

"Find Nilda and Kara," I said. "They can help you."

"I will," she said.

I glanced across the street to where Mjolner still sat perched on the fence post. He gave me a slow wink, and I knew there was more than one way for messages to get to me no matter where I went in the world.

"Come on," I said to Loke, and we headed across town at a faster pace than before.

"Where do you think he is?" Loke asked.

"I don't know," I said. "I can think of a few places. I don't know which, but they all have one thing in common."

"What's that?" he asked.

"He would need someone from Runde to give him a ride to get to any of them," I said.

CHAPTER 12

The bonfire in the cave was banked low again, as it always was when the Thor on duty was patrolling the deeper levels. Loke and I passed through without speaking then carefully made our way down the steep path to the meeting hall.

"You spoke to Roarr already," Loke said.

"Yeah," I said. "First thing yesterday, before I even did the drawings."

"I'm guessing you didn't think he was a suspect, then," he said.

"No, and I don't think I do even now," I admitted. "Taking off is weird, and I definitely want to know what he's up to. But tracking down Raggi before Nilda and Kara did? It kind of sounds like he's running a parallel investigation, doesn't it?"

"If he wanted to help, he should've come to you and just offered to help," Loke said. "Sneaking around is never a good look."

"I don't think Roarr makes the best decisions," I said. "Maybe he did before and grief is still messing him up, I don't know."

"No, he always seemed to have a hard time getting it together," Loke said after a moment's thought. "Lisa was good for him, but she's gone now. So are we heading inside?" he asked as we reached the meeting hall's back patio.

"No, I thought we'd check in with Michelle and Jessica," I said. "If Roarr needed help to get a ride share service to come pick him up, I think he'd do it at the café since its right on the highway."

"Convenience, with a side of avoiding your grandmother," Loke said. I looked over to give him a smile and really noticed for the first time how subtle his clothing choices were. He favored black on black in simple cuts, like someone who didn't want to spend any time doing anything remotely like picking out an outfit. To the extent I'd even thought about it before, I had chalked it up to that blend of laziness and not caring about impressing others that felt very much part of Loke's character.

But now that I was really looking at him as we walked together from one world to another, I saw what had to be his real intent for the first time. His clothing choices were perfectly calibrated to fit in, no matter if he were in Runde or Villmark.

Not that he fit in with the norm in either world. The people of Runde stuck to jeans and flannel and lots of knit caps, and their shirts and jackets varied between up to four different colors. But what at a glance could be taken as black skinny jeans and a loose-fitting black turtleneck wasn't too far outside that norm.

The people of Villmark wore a larger variety of colors and styles in what looked to me like modern reinterpretations of traditional garb, but there his clothes fit in with the other leggings and tunics. I hadn't seen anyone else in Villmark ever wearing all black, but he didn't seem to draw any looks for it.

I wondered how old he had been when he had decided that was his look. Was there an experimental phase?

Trying to picture Loke as an awkward teen almost had me laughing out loud. He shot me a questioning look when I stifled back a sputter of laughter, but I just shook my head. No way was I going to tell him what I was thinking.

We climbed the path up to the level of the highway, emerging behind the garage run by Andrew's father, then crossed the road to the café. There were a few cars parked in the gravel lot, a nice sign considering it was the middle of the week.

"Hey!" Jessica said happily when we entered to the ringing of the bells over her door. "I'll be with you in just a sec."

"We'll be over here," I said, pointing to the computer area. One little cubby already had a customer in it, checking their e-mail while they sipped their coffee and munched on a scone. It wasn't anyone I recognized from Runde, and yet she had an air of someone who had picked her usual spot at her usual time. So Jessica was getting regulars who passed up and down the highway. That was a very good sign.

"I don't think that's going to tell you anything Jessica won't already know," Loke said to me, but I brought up the search history anyway. No one had used it all morning. I moved over to the next computer and did the same. Someone had searched movie showtimes and restaurants in Duluth, but that was it.

"Any news?" Jessica asked as she came out from behind the counter, giving the customer who was heading back out the door with bags of sandwiches a little smile as she passed.

"No, nothing new," I said. "Our other witness said the same as Simon. There was a yacht, too far away to identify, and probably too far away to be involved, anyway."

"So it's a dead end?" She looked even more disappointed than I felt.

"We're working on a side thing," I said. "Maybe not related, but maybe it is. Have you seen Roarr this morning? We think he left town, but since he doesn't drive or have a cellphone, he'd need help to get a ride out here."

"Oh, he didn't have to call anyone," Jessica said. "Andrew was still here when Roarr came in, and he had a car and nothing going on today, so..." she ended with a shrug.

"Andrew drove him?" I asked. Loke already had his phone out of his pocket and jabbed at one of his contacts before putting it to his ear.

"Yeah. It was a while ago, though. They're probably there by now," she said.

"Where?" I asked.

"Duluth," she said, apparently surprised I didn't already know that.

"To watch the boats come and go," I said, mostly to myself, but not so quietly that she didn't hear.

"I don't know about that," she said. "I didn't hear most of what he and Andrew said to each other because I was helping some customers, but it sounded more serious than just sightseeing."

"No answer," Loke said.

"Maybe he's still driving," I said.

"I'm texting him," Loke said.

"You say it looked serious?" I said to Jessica.

"Well, more serious than sightseeing," she said. "Not life or death serious. I don't know for sure. I went to the back to fetch more cream and when I got back out here they were gone."

"In a hurry?"

"More like the conversation was over," she said with a shrug. "Andrew wanted to help, you know. You kind of brushed him off this morning."

"I did not," I objected. "You wanted to come with to talk to Simon. *Someone* needed to stay here."

"If you had left an opening, he would've volunteered," she said.

"So he's not answering calls and texts because he's annoyed with me?" I asked.

"No way," Loke said. "First of all, they're *my* calls and texts. And second of all, that just doesn't sound like Andrew."

"No, I agree. He must still be driving," I said.

"But they must be nearly there by now if they were going to Duluth," Jessica said, turning to look at the clock on the wall behind her. "Even if the weather is different down there, which I don't think it is today."

"What do you want to do?" Loke asked me. "Wait to hear from him?"

"No," I said. "Let's get my car. We can start driving towards Duluth, anyway. Hopefully, we hear from him before we get there so he can tell us exactly where he and Roarr are."

"Call me if you hear anything," Jessica said as we headed back out the door.

We had to wait for a break in traffic to cross the highway, and I found myself looking back over my shoulder, past the café to the lake beyond. I could still feel it, that ever-present pressure against my ears that was somehow stronger when I looked to the lake.

"Loke, do you feel anything?" I asked.

"Feel what?" he asked, eyes still on the traffic.

"Magic, I guess? This feeling like something is about to happen?"

He looked down at me, his dark eyes inscrutable, but all he said was, "something is always about to happen." Then he tugged at my sleeve so I would follow him in jogging across the highway.

My car was parked at the edge of the lot in front of the meeting hall, so we had to take the path back down under the bridge. Loke glanced at his phone from time to time but always tucked it back away again without saying anything.

I hoped Andrew was just being a safe driver. I didn't suppose Roarr would be much help in responding to a text while Andrew was driving.

But I couldn't deny that there was a heaviness in the pit of my stomach, the beginning of a real sense of worry.

I drove around the bluff and took the switchback up to the highway. Then we were on our way south, almost two hours of driving between us and our destination.

"No message?" I asked as I settled back more comfortably into my seat.

"Nothing yet," he said with a little smirk. "Honestly, Ingy, it's not like I could hide it from you if I heard something. You'd hear the same notification I did."

"So we wait," I said amiably. "That gives us lots of time to talk about what's going on with you."

"I'd rather not," he said, turning to look out his side window.

"You've made that very clear," I said. "I'm just not sure it's the best thing for you, letting you shut yourself off like this."

"I'm not shutting myself off," he said, half turning his face back towards me, but not enough to actually make eye contact. "Please, Ingy, can we just ride along in silence?"

"Sure," I said, but I couldn't help adding, "this time."

He let that comment go, and after a moment or two of my not pressing any more conversation on him, he started to relax.

It was a long ride to make in silence, but I was surprised to find it felt companionable, that silence. I didn't feel like I was being prevented from being a support to him in his time of trouble, whatever its cause. Quite the opposite. It was like just being there with him, without a word passing between us, was easing his mind. I didn't know if it was my increased sensitivity to magic or what, but I could sense the tension leaving his mind and body.

But then we reached the outskirts of Duluth, still with no message from Andrew and therefore no idea where to go. Duluth wasn't nearly so large as the Twin Cities where I had grown up, but it was still far too big to just wander around in and hope to stumble across anyone.

"What now? What now?" I asked myself, drumming my fingers on the steering wheel as I pondered the many turns off the highway. Soon we'd be climbing the hill on the far side of town and leave the lake and Duluth both behind us. That would definitely be going too far.

"Lisa went to school here," Loke said. "Maybe that's the best place to start."

"Maybe," I said. "Does it overlook the harbor?"

"No idea," he said, but he was tapping at his phone. "Get off the highway the next chance you get. Just head west and I'll navigate us from there."

"Got it," I said, signaling my turn.

I had never intended to go anywhere but the local art school, so I had never done the visiting colleges thing in high school. I don't think any of my classmates had considered going to college in Duluth either. Even for kids raised in the Twin Cities, it was just too cold that far north and especially right off the lake. I mean, most kids picture college as laying out on the quad, throwing balls and frisbees around and strolling about in shorts. The appeal of a college where the buildings were connected by subterranean passages so the students could avoid the wind and sleet was by definition quite niche.

Still, as we drove past the sign that read Northern College, I was surprised how cozy it all looked. The brick buildings had a warm tone to them, and the trees were holding onto enough of their leaves to make it look more like October than November here. The buildings were arranged in a row, and in between them we could catch glimpses of a gorgeous view of the city and lake below.

"I'm going to find a place to park," I said. "I think we'd have more luck on foot."

"There's a visitors' lot just there," Loke said, consulting his phone as he pointed ahead of us and to the left.

I parked the car, and we both got out. I looked around hopefully, but none of the other cars in the lot were Andrew's.

We walked back the way we'd come to cross the road and get closer to the edge of the bluff beyond the school buildings. There were paved paths everywhere, with benches set under trees every hundred feet or so. Loke nudged my elbow and pointed to a cluster of picnic tables outside of what appeared to be a cafeteria. It was mid afternoon, and only a solitary hearty soul was sitting outside hunched over a book with an enormous travel mug in one of her gloved hands.

"A view of the boats?" I guessed as we walked over to the tables.

"Well, we can see he's not here," Loke said. "But I think you should try a little magic. See if you can draw him to you."

"That's not the kind of drawing magic I do," I said.

"Well, figure out where he is. However it works," he said.

"I'm not even sure if I can," I said. "We're so far from Villmark here."

"You give that a try. I'll try calling Andrew again," he said. I climbed up to sit on the top of the table with my feet on the bench in order to get a better view of the harbor far below.

You really could see the cargo ships from here. One was just getting underway. Further out across the water, another was drawing ever closer.

Well, at the very least, I could get a cool sketch out of this. I took out my book and turned to a blank page, then without further thought just started moving my pencil over the paper.

The process of finishing was like waking from a dream, gradually becoming more aware of the world around me and less lost in my imagination. Loke was sitting on the table beside me now, resting his chin on my shoulder as he examined what I had done.

"Who's the man?" he asked.

At first I didn't understand the question. I had been drawing the cargo ships. The city was sketched out in rough strokes, but the trees closer to me were more finely rendered.

Then I saw, coming up the path between the trees, the outline of a man.

I looked up to see the same path in real life ahead of us, quite empty.

"Was there someone there before?" I asked.

Loke shook his head. "You drew it. Is it Andrew or Roarr?"

I looked more closely at the pencil lines, but I didn't think it was either of them. "Just some random student who passed by?"

"But no one's been there since we got here," Loke insisted.

I traced my graphite-stained thumb over what looked like the silhouette of a hat with earflaps. It was so specific; it *had* to be someone.

Then I looked up again to see someone just coming into view, climbing up that steep path that was really just a deep muddy trench until it met the paved trail that ran parallel to the bluff. They were walking with their head down, hands in pockets, trudging up the nearly vertical slope.

I couldn't see their face, but I was sure I knew that walk.

"Jesús?" I called. But that was impossible. He was hundreds of miles away, back in St. Paul.

And yet the hooded figure looked up at the sound of the name, and I watched his face go from sleepy confusion to startled surprise to surprised joy.

I would know that crooked smile anywhere. It really was Jesús Rodríguez.

CHAPTER 13

I jumped off the picnic table and ran to Jesús nearly as fast as he was running to me. We gave each other a quick hug then stepped back, but I could see I wasn't the only one nearly hopping up and down in excitement. But then Jesús looked over my shoulder at Loke and made a deliberate effort to calm himself down a bit.

"Ingrid Torfa," he said in a mock-accusing tone. "What are you doing here? Some kind of art grad school? Are you teaching?"

"Neither," I said, laughing. "Teaching? I only graduated a couple of months ago."

"Well, I always figured you'd take the art world by storm," he said.

"Not quite," I said.

"Not yet," Loke amended, then stuck out his hand. "I'm Luke."

"Jesús," my old friend said as they shook hands. "Ingrid and I have known each other practically since forever."

"You worked at the diner together," Loke said. I was impressed he had remembered that detail only mentioned in passing on the day we met.

"We did," Jesús said, shooting me a little look that said he was wondering just who Loke was and how much I else I had shared with him.

"Luke is a friend I met when I moved to Runde," I said.

"Oh, that's right!" Jesús said, slapping his own forehead. "I've been trying to remember the name of the town you said you were moving to, but I just kept blanking on it. I wanted to see if I could figure out where you'd gone since you didn't leave a forwarding anything."

"I still have my phone," I said.

"Really?" he asked. "Everything I've tried to send your way has come back undeliverable."

"I'll have to look into that," I said. I suspected that it was related to the magic that hid Villmark somehow. Like Jesús not remembering the name of the town of Runde until I said it.

"Runde is quite a bit north of here, isn't it?" he said with a frown.

"A couple of hours," I said. "We're trying to find someone who came down here. But what are *you* doing here?"

"Oh, me?" he said. "Well, you remember my kid sister Tlalli? Or I guess when you met her she was still going by María."

"Vaguely," I said. "How old is she now? Seventeen?"

"Nineteen," he corrected me. "And she's a student here. She's starting her second year of nursing school. She hated dorm life, so she found an apartment for this year. But then her roommate flaked at the end of the first week, dropped out of school, and left Tlalli high and dry. Well, it's not like I was doing anything much down in St. Paul all by myself, so I packed up and moved up here. I work part time in the cafeteria on campus, plus something closer to full time in a diner off the highway just south of here."

"Like back home," I said.

"Not quite," he said, and the smile on his face faded a touch. "That place was like family."

"It was," I agreed.

We shared a moment of quiet nostalgia, but then he said, "you know, I thought I was coming up here to talk to my boss in the cafeteria, but now that I'm standing here, I can't remember about what."

"Weird, that," Loke said, shooting me a telling look.

"Our apartment is just a little walk down the hill. Do you want to stop in? Tlalli will be getting out of class soon, and I know she'd love to see you again."

I looked at Loke, who just shrugged, but that gleam of mischief was still there in his eye. I knew he was thinking that Jesús didn't remember what he had wanted when he came up the path because *I* had drawn him there. Could that be true? It hadn't felt like I was doing anything but drawing the ships. I hadn't even been thinking about Jesús.

But something had brought us together, most improbably. I had to see if that led to anything, didn't I?

"Let me just grab my stuff," I said, running back to the picnic table and stuffing my sketchpad and pencils back in my bag.

"Still sketching away in every free moment, I see," Jesús said.

"You don't know the half of it," Loke said to him.

We followed Jesús down the muddy track to the sidewalk of a road that ran parallel to the bluff, then up a block to a brick apartment building. Judging by the banners and stickers in the various windows, the entire building was filled with college students. Jesús unlocked the outer door and let us in, but when he brushed past us to lead the way to the apartment, we discovered his sister already there, just unlocking the door with one hand while grasping a stack of mail in the other.

"Tlalli!" Jesús called, and she looked up, startled. "It's Ingrid! You remember Ingrid?"

For a moment, I didn't think she did. But then her eyes lit up. "Oh, from the diner!"

"It's been an age," I said. In truth, I barely remembered meeting her before. She was a lot taller now, and looked more like her brother than she had before. In place of pigtails, her long black hair was pulled back at the nape just like Jesús' shorter ponytail. They had the same dark eyes that were almost black and prominent nose, but her skin was a darker shade of brown than his.

"Well, come in," she said as she pushed the door open and clicked on the lights.

The apartment was tiny but neatly arranged and very clean. There was a kitchenette to one end of the main room, a dining table and chairs dominating the center of the space. A couch was tucked into the far side of the room, angled to allow for looking out the window to the street below as much as to face the tiny television. Both of the bedroom doors were closed, but the one that belonged to Tlalli was easy to spot, decorated as it was with cut-outs of roses and skulls that must have been left over from the Day of the Dead a few days earlier.

"Coffee?" she asked us as she dumped the mail and her book bag onto a chair near the door.

"Yes, please," I said. Loke nodded as well but was distracted by his vibrating phone.

"Do you mind if I take this?" he asked.

"Please," Tlalli said, heading into the kitchenette. Her brother followed her. Despite the tight space, the two of them flowed seamlessly around each other, measuring out water and coffee into the coffeemaker, then taking down mugs and sugar and cream.

Loke crossed the room to the window and turned his back on us, speaking in such a low voice that I couldn't make out a single word. I hovered in the center of the space, not sure if I should try helping in the kitchen - where I'd surely mess up their rhythm - or if I should move closer to Loke so that I could hear or if I should just sit down at the table and wait.

Then Loke turned and waved me over impatiently. I went to stand close to him.

"It's Andrew," he whispered.

"I figured," I said.

"He's here with Roarr, at the school," he said.

"I'm guessing not to look at boats," I said.

"No, Roarr is trying to find some guy he remembers from things Lisa told him," Loke said. "Some guy named Adam Taylor."

I shrugged. The name meant nothing to me. But there was a clatter of a dropped spoon and I turned to see Tlalli watching us both, a stricken look on her face.

"I think she knows that name," Loke stage-whispered to me.

"I do," Tlalli said, not bothering to pretend like she wasn't eavesdropping.

"Andrew says he's bad news," Loke said, pressing the phone closer to his ear. I could hear the rise and fall of Andrew's voice, but only dimly.

"He *is* bad news," Tlalli said.

"Apparently a privileged cad," Loke said, then into the phone. "Tell me that's your words and not Roarr's."

"Privileged cad," Tlalli said, as if rolling the words around in her mouth to see how they felt. "I think that's letting him off lightly."

"Okay, apparently Gullveig met this guy at Lisa's funeral service," Loke said. "I guess he's gotten a little stalkery since."

"Why didn't Roarr tell me this before?" I asked. "Like, when I was talking to him for starters?"

Loke shrugged but held up a finger so I wouldn't interrupt whatever Andrew was saying.

"Is he a stalker type?" I whispered to Tlalli.

"Very," she said, crossing her arms. I think she intended it to look aggressive, but there was something in the tightness of how her fingers gripped her arms. Like she was protecting herself.

"He owns a boat," Loke said, interrupting my thought.

"A boat or a yacht?" I asked.

"A yacht," Tlalli and Loke said at once.

"This is no way to have a conversation," I said. "Can't Andrew and Roarr come to us so we can all talk at once in the same room?"

I looked at Tlalli, and she nodded her permission.

"I'll give him the address," Loke said, moving to the chair by the door to read off the mail left there.

"Do you know this Adam guy well?" I asked Tlalli.

She shifted her weight from foot to foot, and I realized she was very carefully not looking at her brother.

"Tlalli?" he said, concerned.

CATE MARTIN

"They're on their way," Loke said, not realizing he was interrupting. "They've been trying to find this boat down at the harbor, but no luck. They'll be here in a few."

"Tlalli?" Jesús said again, even as he took two more mugs down from the shelf.

"I know him," she said, still looking just at me. "And I know he's a stalker. I came up here to get settled into my apartment a few weeks before school officially started, and I met him at a party. I had seen him around some last year, but never face to face until August. I didn't like his vibe, so I shot down his advances. I thought that'd be the end to it. Who gets obsessed with a girl you talked to for five minutes at a party? A girl who was never, ever into you?"

"Let me guess: Adam Taylor," I said.

"It was a rough few weeks," she said. "He kept turning up everywhere, and that creepy vibe just kept amping up. I can't prove it, but I think he's the reason my roommate bailed. I think he said something to her. Or even did something to her. She left in a hurry and wouldn't really talk to me."

"Tlalli," Jesús said, clearly shocked by this revelation.

"It's why I asked you to move up here," she said, moving to stand beside him so he could put an arm around her. "And he stopped coming by."

"Because of me?" Jesús asked. "Or because he had a new target?"

"It sounds like it times out with meeting Gullveig," I said with a sigh. "Mid September?"

Tlalli nodded. "I was so grateful when he went away. But now I feel bad. I should've known the only reason he would leave off me was because he had a new target. I hope your friend is okay?"

Loke and I exchanged a look. What to say?

"No, she's not," I said. "We don't know if Adam had anything to do with it, but she died a few nights ago."

"Oh!" Tlalli said, pressing a hand to her mouth. "Oh, no!"

"This is not your fault," Jesús told her.

"I feel like it is, though," she said. "I succeeded in driving him away, but I never tried to tell anyone. I never filed a report or anything."

"You must have had a reason," her brother said with unshakeable confidence.

"I did," she admitted. "I know, or know of, five other girls who were his targets in the past. They all tried to have him arrested, or expelled, or get restraining orders against him. It... didn't end well for them. None of them graduated. They just... left."

"Well, this time he's gone so far, something has to happen to him," I said. "We're going to prove what he's done. He's going away for a very long time, I swear it."

"Perfect," Tlalli said. "And we're going to help you."

Her posture was all aggression now, like a warrior on a mission. Her brother beside her had a look on his face that was just as determined.

But could I really involve them? Chasing criminals was dangerous, for one. But also there was the ever-present danger of exposing Villmark to the outside world. If they should somehow learn of its existence, would they keep that secret? Could I ask them to?

Loke was watching me carefully, and I knew he was waiting for me to announce my decision so that he could promptly back it, whatever it was. Either we were all about to plot our next step together, or when Andrew and Roarr arrived, we northerners were going to head right out the door without lingering over coffee.

I tugged my sketchbook back out of my bag and looked at the drawing that had brought Jesús to me. Then I looked up at the siblings waiting for me to accept their offer of help.

"You weren't wearing a hat," I said to Jesús, who touched his thick, dark hair self-consciously.

"No," he admitted. "I just had my hood up. Why?"

But I didn't answer, just looked at Tlalli's things on the chair by the door, reaching under the mail to tug a cap out from out of a side pocket of her backpack.

A knit hat with earflaps ending in long tassels. The pattern was very Nordic, but the bright oranges, reds and blues were pure Mexican. I hadn't conveyed any of that in pencil, but as I held it in my hand, it felt like what I had seen, or sensed, or whatever.

"You *are* going to help us," I said.

I wasn't sure how or why. I just knew that somehow I had needed them, and the universe or perhaps my own power had brought them to me. I couldn't squander that.

"Of course," Tlalli said with a curt nod. "Now, who wants some eggs?"

CHAPTER 14

$\mathcal{B}$y the time Andrew and Roarr arrived, the scrambled eggs I
was cooking on an electric skillet at the dining room table
were almost done. Tlalli was refrying beans she had taken out of a
storage container in the fridge and then mashed by hand, and Jesús
was working right beside her, pressing out fresh corn tortillas and
cooking them one after another on a cast-iron skillet.

"Wow, what's all this?" Andrew asked as Loke led him and Roarr
into the apartment.

"Late lunch," I said. "Or early dinner. Can you help me with the
plates, guys?"

Andrew, Loke and Roarr picked up a plate in each hand and after I
dished up eggs onto each plate, I sent them into the kitchen for beans,
tortillas, and hasty introductions.

Then all six of us crowded around the table that was probably the
right size for two people, but we made it work. At some point when
my back had been turned, Tlalli had whisked away the electric skillet I
had used for the eggs and set out bowls of homemade salsa and
guacamole.

"Thanks for doing this," Andrew said as he forked eggs onto a tortilla with a dollop of beans, then added condiments. "I haven't eaten all day and I'm starving."

"It's quite good," Loke agreed, licking his fingers before loading up another of his tortillas.

"It's just eggs," Tlalli said with a shrug. But she couldn't take her eyes off of Roarr. I could hardly blame her. He had yet to say a word to anyone, but he was shoveling food into his mouth with great gusto. His face was a study of bliss after each new flavor crossed his tongue, and his yummy sounds of appreciation were both loud and frequent.

"I think he likes it," Jesús said with a grin.

"I've never had anything like it," Roarr said. Tlalli's eyebrows furrowed together, like she couldn't work out if he was serious or was playing some kind of joke on them.

"You've never had eggs Tex-Mex style?" she asked.

"No, never," he said, looking wistfully down at his empty plate. She reached over to trade his empty plate for her still half-full one.

"Go on," she said when he tried to refuse her food. "I'm glad you like it. We'll have to have Ingrid bring you by again someday when Jesús and I have more time to plan a real meal for you."

"We'll make you tamales," Jesús promised, raising his eyebrows to communicate how special that was going to be.

"Ugh, tamales," Talli said, pressing a hand over her eyes. "So much work."

"We'll all help," he said to her. "We'll make a day of it."

"That does sound good," she said with a little smile. "I haven't had tamales since..."

She trailed off, but a look passed between the two of them. Whenever they had made tamales last, they were both thinking of the same memory now, and I could tell it was a sad one.

"I would be delighted to accept your invitation," Roarr said. I could tell he was being extra careful with his English pronunciation, although he barely had an accent, and even if it had come through, the siblings would probably just think of it as a Northern Minnesota thing.

"Cooks, stay in your chairs," Loke said as he stood up. "The rest of us can handle the dishes."

"But you're guests," Tlalli said, starting to get to her feet, anyway. He put a hand on her shoulder to keep her in her chair.

"I've got it," he said, giving her his most charming smile. It worked. She sat back and watched as Loke roped Roarr and Andrew into helping him clear the table. I went over to the couch where I had left my art bag and sat down with my sketchbook. I started turning through the last few pages, the ones relevant to our investigation, when I felt Tlalli settling down beside me.

"Ingrid," she whispered to me. I looked up at her. "I don't want to be nosy, but are you dating any of these guys?"

I looked across the room to where Andrew was elbows-deep in dishwater, handing things over to Loke who dried them with the sort of flair that was going to end up in smashed plates if he wasn't careful, especially with Roarr hulking over both of them, trying to find ways to help. I wondered which one she had her eye on. Roarr, who loved even her simplest food? Loke, who had been hitting her with both charm barrels? Or Andrew? He had a quieter appeal.

Had she noticed how fantastic he always smelled?

"No, not dating," I said, hoping my cheeks weren't flushing as pink as it felt like they were. "I'm trying to get my illustration career off the ground, plus I've been helping my grandmother run her business and doing sort of an independent study."

"Too busy for dating," Tlalli said with great sympathy. "I know the feeling. I have to work full time on top of school just to afford all this. I totally get you."

Jesús had been lingering at the dining table, leg bouncing like mad until he gave up his struggle to keep out of the kitchen and hopped up to start directing where clean dishes should go.

"Excuse me for a second," I said to Tlalli, setting my sketchbook aside and crossing the room to Roarr. When I tugged at his sleeve, he was at first relieved to have an excuse to get out of a kitchenette he was way too big for. Then he saw the look on my face.

"Don't look at me like that," he leaned down to whisper to me. "I don't have to report my comings and goings to you."

"I'd think you'd want to," I said. "I'd think you'd want me on your side."

"No, you want *me* on *your* side," he said.

"What's the difference?"

"Who's in charge," he said. "I don't answer to you."

"I'm not trying to boss you around," I said. "But if you know something that could be helpful and you choose not to share it with me, how am I not supposed to feel like you're hiding something from me?"

"I was going to tell you," he said. "When we got back. If it turned out to be anything."

"You had a big lead," I said. "And I have a car. There was no reason to involve Andrew at all."

"Andrew said he was already part of your team," Roarr said.

"You know he can't know everything," I said. "You're making the juggling act I have to do infinitely more complicated."

"I don't think that's on me," he said, tipping his head towards Jesús in the kitchen and then Tlalli, who was sitting on the couch looking through my sketchbook. Judging by the worried frown on her face, I guessed she was looking at my crime scene drawings.

"We're not done discussing this," I said to Roarr, but then hustled back to the couch.

"This is your friend?" she asked, tipping the page towards me.

"Yes," I said. "Two of my friends found her and called me. I saw her before the police took her away. I drew that later from memory."

"Did it help?" she asked.

At first I thought she was asking if drawing it had helped my investigation, which was a strange question to come from someone who didn't know about my magic. But then I realized she thought I had drawn it to get a sense of emotional closure.

"I don't think so," I said. "It's too soon."

"I don't think I've ever seen your art before," she said, handing the sketchbook back to me. "It's a little disturbing. It's like there's more going on than I'm seeing. It's... unsettling."

"This isn't the stuff I'm trying to sell," I said, fighting the urge to flip back to more conventional sketches of trees and cats and the lake. But she must've turned past those pages already.

Jesús plopped down on the couch on the other side of his sister, and Andrew, Loke and Roarr turned the dining room chairs around to face the couch. Then Andrew took his phone out of his pocket and started tapping at the screen.

"So, I've been searching Adam Taylor on the internet, or trying to," he said. "It's a pretty common name."

"He's Adam William Taylor IV, if that helps," Tlalli said. "He has an apartment near here with about four other guys, but his family only lives a few miles north of town."

"One of the palatial estates with the lake in their backyard?" I asked. I had seen them from the highway. Some were mansions, but some bordered on castles.

"Exactly," Tlalli said. "This house is right next to a private marina. His family has a couple of sailboats - yes, you heard me right, more than one - and a yacht. Adam loves to take big groups of college students out on his yacht for parties."

"He has to be our guy," I said. "Too many things are converging here."

"What things?" Tlalli asked.

"Our friend was found washed ashore in Runde, dressed but with no shoes. Two fishing boats that were near there both reported seeing a yacht passing by at the time," I said. "That, plus the very improbable connection between Gullveig, who... didn't get out much, and Adam Taylor. You've met him?" I asked Roarr.

He shook his head. "No, I haven't. I didn't attend Lisa's memorial service."

"So how do you know he met her there?" I asked.

"She told me about it," he said. "Just in passing, and I had forgotten all about it until Raggi told me about seeing the yacht."

"What did she tell you?" I asked.

"It was before that party of yours," he said, searching for the word. "Halloween. About a week before that. He kept texting her, wanting to meet, to take her out somewhere. She stopped by my house one morning to ask me if I remembered Lisa ever saying anything about him. I didn't, really, except I knew he had that boat. Lisa had been to a party on it at some point. That had made an impression on her. But it was a big party, and if she had formed any impression of Adam she hadn't shared it with me."

"Would she have?" Tlalli asked.

Roarr tapped his lips as he thought that over. "I don't know. It would depend on the impression."

"If he creeped her out, she might have kept it to herself," Andrew suggested. "If she didn't want to worry you. If she thought she was able to deal with it herself."

"So Gullveig was asking you about him, like a character reference?" I asked.

"Maybe that was what she was doing," he said, tapping his lip again. "It seemed odd at the time. She had met him and I hadn't, so why ask me what I thought of him?"

"Did she seem worried?" I asked. "Like she was weighing whether or not to meet him?"

"Not worried, no," Roarr said with a little chuckle. "Gullveig could handle herself just fine. But she might have been weighing things, sure."

"And after you said you didn't know him? How did she seem?"

"The same as before. Like I said, it didn't feel like a consequential conversation when we were having it," he said.

"And yet she sought you out specifically to have it," I said.

He shrugged. "If anything I said helped her make up her mind, I didn't see a hint of it when she left."

Which didn't mean that hints weren't there. Roarr seemed to have missed a lot of nuances that just about any other witness could testify to now, but there was nothing to be done about that.

"I can't find an address for his apartment," Andrew said, looking up from his phone. "But I have found his family's house. Should we start there?"

"If we're hoping to find the yacht, that seems like the best option," I said.

"What does finding the yacht gain us?" Loke asked from the kitchen. "We only have the vaguest of descriptions to compare it to."

"If we find any clues on it, that will help," I said. "We can't just give his name to the police without finding more connection than what we have."

Particularly as Roarr, who didn't legally exist in the modern world, wouldn't be able to testify to any of it.

"We're going to sneak into a private marina and sneak onto a private vessel, to snoop around?" Andrew asked.

"Well, I thought we'd stop by the house first and see if he's home and will talk with us," I said. "But if that doesn't pan out, yeah. Snooping is called for."

"Snooping sounds like a good Plan B to me," Tlalli said, clapping her hands together. "Let's go."

CHAPTER 15

A thick stand of evergreens stood between the highway and Adam's family's house on the lake, so thick I couldn't even see the house from the tiny bit of driveway we could pull into before having to stop at a gate. Andrew's car was in front of me, and I saw him press a button on a talk box, but it was Tlalli who leaned over him from the backseat to speak to whoever was on the other end.

"I wonder what she's saying," I said to Loke.

"She's your friend," he said.

"Not really," I admitted. "I've only met her a couple of times. She's quite a bit younger than Jesús, and he and I never really hung out besides at work, anyway. I mean, we both worked a lot of hours, usually together. But I don't know her well at all."

"I like her," Loke said as if that settled the matter.

"Yeah, I think I do too," I said.

I had no idea what she said, but I wasn't entirely surprised when the gates swung open and first Andrew and then I drove through, following the curving driveway down the slope of a hill until first the lake and then an immense brick mansion came into view.

"Quaint," Loke said. "Cozy little place. What do you think, just twelve bedrooms?"

"These people own a yacht they are willing to let their son take out for parties without their supervision," I said as I pulled up beside Andrew and shut off the car. "I don't think wasting money is something they worry about much."

As Loke and I got out of the car, we realized we were catching the others in mid conversation.

"What's going on?" I asked.

"Tlalli wants us to say here," Jesús told me.

"I don't think that's a good idea," Andrew said. "We should stick together."

"If all six of us turn up on the doorstep, their housekeeper is going to freak out," Tlalli said. "I think it should be just me and Ingrid."

"What did you tell her?" I asked.

"I told her that my friend is Adam's girlfriend and she left something in his room the last time she was here," Tlalli said. "That's you, by the way. You're the girlfriend."

"Who's going to believe that?" I asked.

"I can sell it," Tlalli said, looping her arm through mine. "But the guys have to stay here. We're just two friends retrieving a thing of personal significance. We don't need a gang."

"Ingrid-" Andrew started to say.

"No, I think she's right," I said. "We just want to have a look around, right? This makes sense. He's not home, is he?" I asked Tlalli.

"No, she's not seen him at all today," Tlalli said.

"You four can be lookout, and we'll call if we run into any trouble," I said. "If he's not here, this is our best chance at snooping."

"Fine. We'll wait here," Andrew said, but I could tell that he hated it.

"What are we going to do when she doesn't recognize me?" I whispered to Tlalli as we climbed the steps to the front door.

"Adam goes through a lot of girlfriends," she whispered back. "Even if she doesn't know you, she'll just think you're one of the many she never met."

"I hope you're right," I said. It was too late to back out now; she had already rung the doorbell.

"Hello!" Tlalli said with a big smile before the door was even all the way open. The woman on the other side was dressed in jeans and a pale blue sweater set and was wearing soft house shoes. Her salt and pepper hair was drawn back in a neat bun, and she was wearing discrete pearl earrings, although I doubted they were real pearls.

Even so, she seemed more the sort of housekeeper who supervised cleaners than one who cleaned herself, and she didn't look pleased at the idea of letting us inside her employer's immaculate house.

"You are Adam's girlfriend?" she asked, looking Tlalli over.

"No, my friend Ingrid here," Tlalli said, pulling my arm to draw me closer to her side. I pulled the wool cap off my head as if that was going to reveal my identity.

Now she looked me over and frowned. "His girlfriend is taller with blonde hair."

"Ugh, that's the new girl," Tlalli said. "He broke *my* girl's heart, and right on her birthday. Can you believe it?"

"Yes," she said. Her mouth stayed as dour as ever, but I could see the hint of a smile in her eyes just before she stepped back to let us inside. "Yes, that I can believe."

"It was upsetting at the time, but she's doing better now," Tlalli went on as we stepped inside the immense front hall. Not one but two staircases led up to the upper floor, curving around either side of the marble-floored foyer. A chandelier hung over the center of the space, directly over a marble-topped table that held a huge arrangement of fresh flowers.

But it felt cold, that place. Perhaps because all the lights were off, leaving just the grayish light from the lake to barely stream through the stained glass windows that adorned the second floor landing. It was the opposite of inviting. Like it was a house, not a home.

Tlalli was giving me a pointed look, and I realized she wanted me to fill in the gap in the conversation. I cast my mind back to what she had just said, then offered what I hoped was an appropriately wavering smile for the housekeeper. "Yes, I'm doing better."

"There's no use hoping he'll take you back," she warned me. "He never does."

"No, I know it's over," I said. "And you know, maybe I'm better off. He felt like trouble to me."

The housekeeper snorted and nodded but said nothing. I longed to pin her down and draw out the details, but Tlalli had other ideas.

"We're just here for Ingrid's grandmother's locket," Tlalli said. "She lost it when she was here, maybe up in his room?"

"You said it was lost at a party," the housekeeper said with a frown.

"It was *during* a party," Tlalli said, "but she knows she had it when she went upstairs with Adam. And then she left the house, because... well."

"Gullveig," I said. "That's when he met Gullveig."

"Yes, that's the girl's name," the housekeeper said, as if I had triggered a memory. "Such an odd one. You both can't remember it, and yet can't mistake it once you've heard it. You know?"

"Exactly," Tlalli said. Then gave a worried frown. "Are you expecting him back soon? Because that might be awkward."

"No, I don't think so," she said. "But do be quick."

"Are his parents coming home?" I asked.

"No, but I feel a storm coming," she said, drawing her sweater more closely around her. "A bad one. You'll want to be safely home before it breaks."

"We'll hurry," Tlalli promised, catching my arm to pull me up the stairs. I looked out through the clear panes in the stained glass windows on the landing, but the clouds over the lake were the same as ever. I could feel the pressure on my ears, but no worse than before.

Still, it felt like the housekeeper had been speaking truth to me. She felt a storm coming, and I didn't doubt that, whether she got her information magically or just had a feeling in her joints or what, she was right.

A storm was coming.

"Come on," Tlalli said, pulling me down the hall towards the front of the house.

"How do you even know which room is his?" I asked.

"The parents will have the room overlooking the lake, right?" she said.

"Probably," I said.

"And that one there is the only other door that's closed," she said, pointing to the last door down the hall ahead of us. "So the rest of these are just guest rooms."

"Good thinking," I said.

I was a little worried that the door might be locked, but the handle turned easily at my touch and we were inside. I closed the door behind us, then flicked on the lights.

Like the rest of the house, it didn't feel like a room anyone actually lived in. There was nothing set out on the top of the dresser or the nightstand, and the bookshelf had the uniform color patterns of someone who bought sets of books and shelved them without ever cracking them open.

"Maybe we went to the wrong place," I said.

"No, this is his room," Tlalli said confidently.

"I mean, maybe anything like a clue is going to be at his apartment, not here," I said.

"He has roommates there," Tlalli said. "College roommates are snoops. No, if there's anything important, he'll keep it here."

"But clearly someone cleans this room for him," I said, sweeping my foot over the neatly vacuumed carpet.

"Someone who is paid to mind their own business," she said. "Let's get going. We have to be quick."

We split up and started pulling open drawers. I ran my hands over neatly folded clothes and carefully arranged toiletries, but there was nothing that showed any particular personality at all.

Tlalli sat down at his desk and started going through drawers of what looked like untouched stationary and writing supplies. I stepped into the private bathroom.

The bedroom windows overlooked the front lawn and the thick row of evergreen trees, but the window over the large bathtub over-looked the side of the house. I could see more lawn and what looked like an English garden with hedges and shrubs now covered in protective canvas for the winter. But beyond that I could just see the lake, and the darkening skies over the lake.

My ears started to ring, and the pressure was suddenly so intense I felt like my eardrums were about to burst. I closed my eyes and took deep breaths until the feeling finally passed. When I opened my eyes, I saw my hands gripping the edge of the sink so intensely they had gone white.

"Ingrid? Everything okay in there?" Tlalli called as she slammed shut a drawer.

"Yeah," I said. "I'm not finding anything, though. You?"

"Nothing yet," she said.

I looked up at my face in the mirror, then swung open the medicine cabinet door. It was more of the same generic toiletries and I started to swing it shut again when something dark orange caught my eye.

A prescription bottle?

I opened the door again and grabbed the bottle. It looked legit, with a label cluttered with warning symbols and reminders to read the accompanying instructions for dosage and side effect information. But what kind of prescription drug would a young man be taking? Something for depression or anxiety, maybe? But was it relevant to what happened, or just a random thing?

I looked more closely at the name on the label.

"What's flunitrazepam?" I called out to Tlalli even as I pulled out my phone and tapped the letters into the search bar. She was, after all, studying to be a nurse.

"Rohypnol," she said, suddenly standing in the bathroom doorway. "That's his prescription?"

"His name is on it," I said. "It says it's for insomnia?"

"That would be the only thing you could get it prescribed for," she said, her face grave. "But even if he has insomnia, this isn't the usual course of treatment. It's very irregular."

"So as a rich boy he doesn't need to get his illicit drugs from criminal channels," I guessed. "He just finds a doctor willing to write him the prescription, no questions asked."

"It certainly looks that way," she said.

I looked at the bottle in my hand. It looked so innocuous. Innocent, even. Like so much aspirin he kept on hand in case he got a headache. "Are there any rumors about him and stuff like this? Anything at all?" I asked.

"No," she said with great reluctance. "Not that I've ever heard. And I've been digging into him for a while. I've talked to every ex-girlfriend or past stalking victim I could find, but none of them ever mentioned anything like this."

"Maybe he's upped his game," I said, and started to put the bottle in my jacket pocket.

"You should put that back," she said.

"So he can use these on some other girl?" I asked. Of course, what I really wanted to do was sit down with the bottle and my sketchbook and see what emerged, but I couldn't tell her that.

"He'll just get a refill when he wants it," she said. "Plus, if we find anything we can actually go to the police with, we'll want that there where we found it so they can find it too."

"With my fingerprints all over it," I said, wiping the bottle against the front of my pants. I wasn't sure if that would work or not. "I don't know what more we can possibly find to give to the police. Not without an awkward explanation about how we found it. Maybe we should leave an anonymous tip about this?"

"Maybe," she said slowly. "But let's leave that as a last resort. In the meantime, I did find one thing to show you."

"What's that?" I asked, holding the bottle with my hand in my sleeve to put it back in the cabinet. I tried not to think about how my fingerprints and Tlalli's were already all over everything else.

"Take a look at this," she said, waving me over to a small table between two chairs under the bay windows. Resting on the table was a framed photograph. I leaned down to get a better look without touching it. "One of his famous yacht parties, I'm guessing?" I said. There were more than a dozen people crowded into the shot. Young men with arms around each other, cheeks already bright from whatever was in the coolers at their feet. Young women striking poses, the photo snapped at the split second before they burst out into laughter. "I don't see Gullveig."

"No, but look at what you can see," Tlalli said.

"The name of the boat," I said, squinting at the letters just visible in the corner of the shot.

"*Fortune's Fool*," Tlalli said. "That's a lead, right?"

"I should say so," I agreed. "Let's go get the boys. I think we should head down to that private marina."

CHAPTER 16

*W*e went downstairs and found the housekeeper still lingering in the front hall. She started to speak, but the words were lost to me as the ringing in my ears came back with a vengeance. Tlalli gave me a concerned looked, but then rushed forward to talk with the housekeeper. She kept the older woman's attention focused on her and not on me stumbling down the last few steps as a wave of vertigo washed over me.

I made it to the marble floor with a lot of help from the bannister, but then faced the prospect of walking without assistance across the space between the bottom of the stairs and the door to the outside world.

It seemed untraversable.

"She's just upset," I heard Tlalli say, but garbled as if through a speaker at the bottom of a pool. She continued speaking, but I lost the thread again. I just knew she was looping her arm through mine to guide me to the door.

"... should call...?" was all I gathered from what the housekeeper was saying.

"No, we have friends waiting. We'll take care of her. She's just so overwhelmed," Tlalli said. The ringing and pain were subsiding, but the queasy vertigo feeling was lingering.

"Thank you," I said, I hoped in the direction of the housekeeper.

Then we were outside in the cold November air. For a moment it was wonderful, the chill snapping me awake faster than the strongest cup of coffee ever could.

But it quickly became too cold, and I extracted my arm from Tlalli's so that I could get my wool cap out of my pocket as well as my gloves.

"Are you all right?" she asked, leaning in to get a closer look at my face. "I thought at first you were doing an act, but you weren't, were you?"

"I'm fine now," I said.

"You're very pale," she said.

"It's okay," I said. "Please, don't say anything to Andrew. He's inclined to worry, and there's nothing to worry about."

"Not a word to Andrew, but Loke is okay?" she asked with a quirk to one side of her mouth.

"It's a long story," I said. "But you've got the gist of it."

"I guess I do," she said. "But at some point I'd love to make the time to hear the whole thing."

"Sure," I said, mustering up a grin.

No way was I ever going to be able to tell her the whole thing.

But then we reached the corner of the house and could see the lake behind it. The skies were gray, but no more ominous than before. If a storm was building, the only thing saying so was my ears.

But Tlalli was looking that way too, with a frown to match my own.

I wanted to ask what she was thinking, but the guys had seen us coming and walked out to meet us halfway across the driveway.

"We're heading to the marina," Tlalli said, waving her hands for them to get back to the cars.

"She's in charge now?" Loke asked.

"No one's in charge," I said to him. "But yes, we're heading to the marina. We know the name of the yacht now. There might be more clues there."

"More clues?" Andrew asked. He looked at me with that worried line between his eyebrows, and I knew he was going to tell me that I didn't look well. But to my surprise he just asked, "What did you find?"

"Maybe something, maybe nothing. Tlalli can tell you on the way," I said.

"We're splitting up again?" he asked.

"Just for the drive," I said. "It's your car and my car. I don't see how the two of us can both go in one."

"You don't look good," he said, clearly not able to hold back that thought any longer.

"Thanks," I shot back, with a bit more aggravation than I intended. He actually flinched, and I felt like the meanest person in the world. I took a deep breath and tried again. "I'm fine. But we really should get going."

"Is he getting away?" Roarr asked.

"We don't know where he is," Tlalli said. "But the weather is about to change. We need to move quickly."

"The weather looks fine," Andrew said. He wasn't looking out over the lake, though. He was scrolling through a forecast on his phone, then tapping a button to take him to a radar screen. "Clear all afternoon into the evening."

"I'm with Tlalli. We should get going," I said and opened my car door.

"Do you need me to drive?" Jesús asked.

"You have a license?" I asked, surprised at that news.

"Well, no," he admitted. "But you don't look good."

Like I needed to hear that again. "I'll be fine," I said through gritted teeth.

"Tlalli, I'm riding with Ingrid and Loke," Jesús called out to his sister, who gave him a thumbs up. He gave me one more look that told him he was not convinced I was anything like fine, but then he got into the back seat.

"They aren't wrong," Loke whispered to me over the roof of the car.

"Don't you feel it?" I asked, waving a hand towards the lake. He shook his head. "Something is about to shift," I said.

He leaned halfway across the roof of my little car and just barely mouthed the word, "magic?"

"It doesn't feel like anything I've ever sensed before," I said. "But do you want to know the weirdest thing? I think Tlalli feels it too."

Loke frowned at me, then looked over his shoulder at where Tlalli was sitting in Andrew's back seat giving him directions as she consulted her phone. Andrew nodded, checked his mirrors, then caught my eye. He gave me a little salute, then backed up to turn around and head up the hill towards the highway.

We headed back towards Duluth, but then turned off the highway again almost immediately, heading down another narrow, tree-lined driveway towards the lake. This driveway ended in an empty parking lot. I could see a few yachts lined up along the docks, but most of the boats were already stacked in a storage facility on the south side of the marina.

And it was all behind a security fence, inaccessible save through the manned gatehouse. The guard inside had a television on but was currently standing up and watching us as we piled out of our cars.

"No sneaking past him, I guess," Loke said. "Do we have a story?"

"Story? Come on," Tlalli said, throwing an arm around him. "We're here for the party!"

"A party? Today? No one is ever going to believe that," Loke said.

"Rich boys don't let paltry things like the weather hold them back," she said, then turned to walk across the lot to the gatehouse. Loke shrugged then followed her, Jesús and Roarr in step behind him.

Andrew came around the front of my car to me before I had shut my door. "Tlalli told me about the drug you found," he said. "Isn't that enough?"

"Is it the same thing that was found in her bloodstream?" I asked.

"I don't know," he admitted. "Do you know who would know? The police."

"How are we going to explain how we found it?" I asked.

"Tell them the whole story," he said. "Starting with Roarr seeing this guy talking to Gullveig at Lisa's service."

"Roarr can't talk to the police," I said, and immediately regretted it.

"Why can't Roarr talk to the police?" Andrew asked, his eyes narrowing with suspicion.

"It's hard to explain," I said. "He just can't."

"Maybe that should be his decision and not yours," Andrew said.

"It is his decision," I said. Then I looked towards the gatehouse. I could see Tlalli in full party girl in search of a party mode, a particularly impressive bit of acting as she was in no way dressed for a party. But the guard didn't look like he was buying it. "I need to be over there," I said to Andrew, but I didn't wait for him to respond before jogging over to the others.

"But I *know* he said today!" Tlalli was pleading.

"And yet, no one is here throwing a party," the guard said with a shrug.

"He left without us," Loke said suddenly. "Didn't he? Look, Tiffany. There's where the yacht should be. That big gaping hole just there." He pointed out at a random spot of water next to the dock. Tlalli, apparently currently employing the name Tiffany, pulled an only slightly exaggerated pout.

"If it helps, the party didn't leave without you," the guard said, clearly taking pity on her.

"What do you mean?" she asked.

"That kid left this morning," he said. "Not a day I'd pick to be out on the lake, but I'm the guard, not the nanny." He scowled in a way that communicated a feeling that the kid in question was definitely in need of said nanny.

"But he was alone?" Tlalli asked, still with a hint of a pout.

"Totally and completely," the guard said. "If there ever was a party, he definitely called it off. Now it's time for you all to shove off. This is private property."

"Okay," Tlalli said. "But thanks for the help."

"Meh," the guard said, waving us away from his window so he could get back to his show.

We headed back across the parking lot to our cars. I saw that Andrew had never left the spot where he had been standing talking to me. He was still there, hunched over his phone.

"The boat's gone," Loke told him as we gathered in a huddle around my car.

"I figured by how it seemed to be going," he said, still engrossed in his phone. "This is maddening. I'm going to set up a hot spot and use my computer for this."

"For what?" I asked.

He looked up at me with an almost Loke-like grin. "Come on and I'll show you."

We all followed him to his car as he reached into the backseat for his backpack and slid out his laptop. It took a minute to get connected, a very long minute since we were out in the wind so close to the lake. Then he tapped away at the keyboard for another maddeningly long minute before turning it around in his hands to show us all the screen.

"Nice map of the lake," Loke said, clearly not impressed.

But it was more than a map. "Those dots," I said, hovering a fingertip over a cluster of pink icons.

"Zoom in," Jesús said. Andrew turned the computer back around to do so, then turned it to face us again.

"Is that every ship out on the lake right now?" I asked.

"Not *every* ship," he conceded.

"It looks like every cargo ship," Jesús said, indicating the various points that pretty much defined the line of the transport lane that led out of Duluth.

"And fishing vessels, here," I said, pointing closer to the north shore.

"Just commercial boats, then?" Tlalli asked.

"No, there are others as well," Andrew said. "See this one here, just south of Isle Royale?"

"It says personal craft," I said. "Is someone identifying that from orbital satellite data, then?"

"For that vessel, yes," Andrew said. "But any vessel can send their information if they want their ship name and port of origin or whatever to appear."

"If Adam is out on the water in his family's yacht, then he's fleeing a crime," Tlalli said.

"We don't know that for a fact," Andrew said.

"We kind of do," she shot back.

"If he's hiding, then he's not sending the extra information, right?" I guessed. "We'd have to go through every icon on this map and look at everything that might be a yacht and find one with no name listed."

"How?" Jesús asked. "It's not like we can zoom in and get live satellite footage or anything. Wait, can we?" he asked Andrew. Andrew shook his head.

"So how does this help us?" Roarr asked.

"We know Adam isn't here," I said. "We know he took his yacht out and hasn't come back. But is he hiding or fleeing?"

"Fleeing?" Roarr asked with a frown.

"To Canada," Tlalli said. "Can he do that?"

"Right now? When he's not even a suspect? Why would anyone stop him?" I said.

"Do any of those boats look like they're going to Canada?" Jesús asked.

"It's hard to say," Andrew said. "We have to figure out which icons represent ships that could be his. Then we'd have to watch what they do over time."

"We're going to be standing here how long?" Loke asked, hands buried deep in his pockets. As usual, he had no hat or gloves.

"Not here," Andrew said. "I'll keep the phone set up as a hot spot and someone can ride in the backseat to keep an eye on the computer. But I think in the meantime we should drive back to Runde."

"To Runde?" Tlalli repeated.

"We need to get a boat," he said. "We need to be out on the water to find this guy. I don't know if any of us can afford to rent a boat from here, or if that's even an option in November. I'm pretty sure none of us have boating experience." We all shook our heads, even Roarr. "Well, I know people in Runde who have the skills and will be eager to help. So we should head that way now."

"Especially if he's trying to flee," Tlalli said. "It's a long drive and we're losing time even while we're standing here."

I took a step away from the others to look out over the lake. The clouds were the same. The water was the same, not calm but nothing like dangerous. Still, I couldn't shake the feeling that something was coming.

"Ingrid?" Tlalli called.

"I agree," I said, turning away from the lake. "Time is short. We should get you two back to your apartment and then head north with all speed."

"You know what's even faster? Just taking us with you," she said. Jesús nodded firmly.

"It's a long drive," I said. "And despite what Andrew's phone app says, I'm worried about the weather. If there's a storm, you could get stuck up north with us for who knows how long."

"We'll be fine," she said. "We're with you until the end on this."

"At this point, not meeting this guy at least once isn't really an option," Jesús said.

"But work and school?" I said.

"Can wait," he said. "Hey, do you know what would be more efficient? Continuing this argument in the car. On the way north to Runde."

"Fine, no argument," I said, raising my hands in surrender. "Let's get on the road."

"I'll man the computer," Tlalli said, taking the laptop from Andrew so he could move to the driver's seat of his car.

"See you when we get there," I said. He caught my hand and gave it a squeeze. Then he got into his car and I got into mine.

"So, Jesús," Loke said as I started pulling out of the parking spot to get back onto the highway. "Tell me the story of your life."

CHAPTER 17

*I*t quickly became embarrassing, how little I knew about Jesús.

I mean, I knew he was funny. He could do things with his face that didn't seem humanly possible and was a spot-on mimic.

I knew he was a hard worker, but an easy-going coworker. He could be the only cook working a shift that really needed three cooks and never fall behind or even seem stressed. And that calmness was contagious. Like he could just make everyone's stress evaporate the same as his own.

I knew he liked to read comic books, whether superhero or horror or graphic tellings of literary classics. He always had a stack in his backpack, in English and Spanish both, ready for any opportunity to dive in for even just a few minutes.

But, as it turned out, there was so much I didn't know.

"So wait," I said, interrupting for what felt like the hundredth time. "When you took a month off every summer to visit your grandmother, you were going to Mexico City? And it wasn't just your grandma, it was your mother too? Because she lived there, not with you?"

"Where did you think I went?" Jesús asked, more amused than offended by the gaps in my knowledge.

"I don't know, Texas?" I said. "You don't have an accent."

"I did before I met you," he said. "Kids are mean. Anybody with an accent in elementary school learns how to sound local as quick as they can, trust me. And sounding like a Texan up here would've been just as bad as sounding Mexican."

"Ingrid is learning a lot about being the new kid these days," Loke said.

"Me too, again. Duluth isn't the same as St. Paul. But how's it going with you?" Jesús asked.

"I'm still working on the accent," I said, and out of the corner of my eye I could see Loke covering a smile with his hand. Technically, it was an accent in a whole other language, but it was still true. "But wait, are your parents still married then? Because you only ever talked about your dad, so I assumed they were divorced."

"Ah," Jesús said, as if collecting his thoughts. "My mother passed about seven years ago. So before I met you. But it was still raw, so I didn't talk about her."

"So you really were visiting your grandma," I said.

"Ah," he drawled again, rubbing at his chin as if checking the closeness of his shave.

"You don't have to tell me things if they make you uncomfortable," I said. My own mother had died months before, after a nearly lifelong illness, but still. I missed her daily.

After seven years his grief might not be as raw, but it would still be there. Or so I told myself, because the real impression I had was that he was trying to very carefully word his answers around a secret without revealing there even was a secret. Like I did when I talked around the matter of Villmark. And yet, why would he do that?

"No, it's okay," he said. "My father brought Tlalli and I here when I was in the third grade and she was still a preschooler, because he got his engineering job at one of the big agricultural firms here. But my mother stayed behind in Mexico City."

"Why?" Loke asked.

"She had reasons," Jesús said vaguely.

"Are those reasons anything to do with why your sister's name is Tlalli now and not María?" Loke asked.

I shot him a questioning look, and he gave me a little shake of his head, warning me not to interrupt. But before Jesús could answer, my cellphone rang.

"Ingrid's phone," Loke said after picking it up out of the cupholder and turning on the speakerphone. "We're all here, though. What's up?"

"Hello, Loke," Roarr said with careful politeness. "There has been a change in the map on the computer."

"What kind of change?" I asked, leaning slightly towards the middle of the car to be sure my voice was picked up on the mic. We could hear the murmur of Tlalli's voice explaining something in the other car, but she was too far away to make out the words.

"Do you remember the ship we saw that appeared to be anchored south of Isle Royale?" he asked.

"Sure. The unnamed one?" I asked.

"Exactly," Roarr said. "It is no longer stationary. It is going north, towards..." He broke off and Tlalli spoke again. Then he repeated her words, "Thunder Bay." Then added under his breath, "good name."

"Thunder Bay," I said. "Canada."

"Yes, that's correct," Roarr said. Now it was Andrew's voice we could hear speaking unclearly in the background. It seemed that Roarr did not have us on speakerphone. "Andrew says he believes this may be due to the weather. If so, if this ship is trying to reach a safer harbor, they may start *pinging* their information to the... map people," he trailed off uncertainly. The word "pinging" had been a touch too foreign for him as well.

"The weather?" Jesús said, moving to the right-hand side of the backseat to look out at the gray sky over the lake. "I guess that might be rain out there."

"Rain and waves," Loke said, also pressing his forehead to the glass of his window. Then he turned to me. "Is this what you were feeling, do you think?"

"I don't know," I said. I could still feel the pressure against my ears. It waxed and waned without ever quite going away.

Or getting intensely worse, as it had before. I didn't want to think what would happen if I had another attack like that while driving.

"Roarr, there's nothing we can do until we get back home," I said towards the phone. "I don't think it's even safe to try to get there faster."

"Andrew says absolutely not," Roarr said.

"Of course he does," I said under my breath. Then, more loudly, "we're going to let you go, but call again if anything changes. Especially if that name pops up. Be sure Tlalli is watching the whole map. It's always possible that isn't the boat we're looking for."

There was the muffled sound of people speaking away from the microphone, and then Roarr was back. "She is doing so already. Andrew wants to know if you have any other instructions?"

"No," I said. "But I'm going to have Luke make some calls from here."

"Okay," Roarr said. "Andrew says to drive safely."

"Always do," I said, then Loke hung up the phone.

"That guy is a riot," Jesús said with fondness. "Is he for real?"

"What do you mean?" I asked.

"He sounds so formal when he says certain things," he said. Then, in an eerily accurate mimic of Roarr's voice, he said, "Thunder Bay, Canada. Good name."

Loke laughed out loud.

"That's just an accent thing," I said. "Small northern town, you know?"

"If you say so. But it's like I could picture him holding a cellphone like he's never seen one before in his life," Jesús said. "And the way he was looking at Andrew's laptop in the parking lot. Like it was an inexplicable marvel of some alien technology."

"It's a small town," I said. "A very, very small town."

"I've been to some small towns in my day," Jesús said amiably. "They all had Mexican restaurants."

"Well, you'll see what I mean in about half an hour," I said.

Although with the darkening skies, I was starting to worry we'd be delayed.

"I'm making calls?" Loke said to me.

"Yes, please," I said. "Call Jessica and Michelle. They are in my contacts. Tell them we need anyone with a boat who can take us out on the lake as soon as we get there. And then have them go to the meeting hall."

"To meet us, presumably?" Loke said as he scrolled through the few contacts on my phone.

"Hopefully with a boat person, yes," I said. There was a sudden burst of wind blowing in from the lake, strong enough to start to nudge the car over into the lane of oncoming traffic, but I didn't let it. The next blast of wind brought the rain with it, and I switched on my headlights and turned the wipers on at their highest setting. "And have them tell my grandmother everything they know. Save me some time when I get there."

"I'll have to fill them in first," Loke said as he pressed the call button then brought the phone up to his ear.

"I know," I said. "I just hope they can find someone who will take us out in this."

"If he gets to Canada, does it really matter?" Jesús asked. "If he's charged here, he'll be extradited. I don't care who his daddy is."

"Unless he opts to keep moving, to some country where he *can* disappear. Some country without extradition treaties with us," I said.

"Those aren't great places, for the most part," Jesús said.

"Jessica didn't answer," Loke told me as he scrolled through my contacts again. "I'm going to try Michelle."

"Okay," I said. "Failing that, do you have anyone else you can call?"

"In Runde?" he asked me.

I bit my lip, fighting the urge to lean forward over the steering wheel as if that would make the car go any faster. Or make the road ahead clearer.

Which was more obscured to me, the road in front of the car being lashed with sheets of rain? Or the metaphorical road ahead of me?

The one that I couldn't even tell if I was meant to walk alone or with my friends?

And how many friends? Loke always felt like he belonged by my side, because he also belonged to both worlds. But what about Andrew? Roarr? Jessica and Michelle? Jesús and Tlalli?

They were all eager to help, but accepting that help meant putting them at risk. Worse, they were taking risks I couldn't possibly define for them. They wouldn't know until it was too late just what they had signed up for.

"Ingrid?" Loke said, calling my mind back to the inside of the car.

"In Runde," I said, settling back into my car seat, although my body refused to loosen any of the tension.

"Because if you need more help-" Loke started to say.

"We both know I can call for it," I cut him off. "Anytime. I've done it before. I can do it again."

"But you don't want to be a bother," he said with that sly grin back on his face.

"*He* is hard to explain, isn't he?" I hissed at Loke.

Loke looked confused for a moment, but then gave a little nod. "That he is," he agreed, then whispered, "for a minute there I thought you were dropping all the veils. So to speak."

"I will if I have to," I said.

"Do you feel like you have to?" he asked.

"I don't know," I admitted.

Then he leaned across the center console to whisper even more softly, close to my ear. "Do you feel like that's your call?"

"If I feel like I have to do it, in that moment, it's going to be my call," I said.

Loke sat back and turned his attention back to my phone in his hand. "Interesting to know," he said, then pushed the button to call Michelle.

"I'm guessing you're not going to tell me what you're talking about," Jesús said.

"It's complicated," I said.

"I'm starting to get that impression," he said. "That's okay. I get complicated. I can go with that flow." I was about to thank him when he added, "Tlalli on the other hand?"

"She's going to demand answers?" I guessed, glancing at his reflection in my rearview mirror.

"Probably not," he said with a little shrug. "No, Tlalli has a way of just digging answers up on her own."

"Great," I said drily.

Clearly job one when we reached Runde was to pull my grandmother aside. I *so* needed a little guidance.

CHAPTER 18

*a*s I feared, it took nearly twice as long as it should have to reach Runde. The wind grew stronger with each gust, always trying to push my little car over into the next lane, and the rain was so dense the visibility was down to mere feet. I had to slow to a crawl, following a safe distance behind what I recognized as the bumper of Andrew's car. Luckily, almost no one else was out driving in this weather. We pretty much had the road to ourselves.

Finally, we reached the turnoff for Runde. The hairpin turn on the dirt road overlooking the lake shore was scarier than usual, and I took it a lot slower than Andrew did. By the time I reached the bottom of the hill, his tail lights were nowhere to be seen.

I pulled into a spot at the back of the meeting hall parking lot and shut off the car. I hadn't realized how tightly I had been gripping the steering wheel until I tried to let it go.

"So this is Runde," Jesús said, his forehead pressed against the glass. There was absolutely nothing to be seen through the rain. Even the meeting hall on the other end of the parking lot was lost in darkness.

"Yeah, this is home," I said. "Ready to make a run for it?"

"You bet," he said, snugging his cap a little lower on his head before pulling up the hood of his windbreaker.

We all three jumped out of the car at once, slamming the doors and racing over the loose gravel and around the already deep puddles towards the light from the open door of the meeting hall.

"Hello!" my grandmother said as we raced past her. "Shake off the water here on the mat, please. Hang your coats by the space heater there. Then you can join the others for a mug of something hot."

I stomped my feet and shook the rain off my coat before taking it off and hanging it from the back of a chair near the space heater. Jesús carefully did the same.

Loke, for whatever reason, didn't even appear to be wet. I decided against calling any attention to that, and instead crossed the room to where Andrew, Roarr and Tlalli were gathered around another space heater, accepting mugs off a tray that Michelle held out to them. It would be a lot warmer inside the meeting hall once it was the mead hall with its massive fireplace.

"Hot chocolate," Michelle said as she turned the tray until the three mugs that remained on it were facing us. "We've been expecting you for a while now."

"Yeah, the rain," I said, taking one of the mugs. There was a hefty dollop of fresh whipped cream on top, and I could smell cinnamon and nutmeg with just a hint of ginger. But at the moment it just felt good to have something warm in my hands and to feel the steam on my face when I breathed in the aroma. I sat down on one of the chairs and took a sip that was more cream than chocolate.

"This place," Tlalli leaned over to whisper to me, her voice full of awe. "This place is amazing. Just amazing."

"Really?" Andrew said, looking around as if seeing the place with new eyes. But it looked the same as it always did by day: dingy and drab, everything showing signs of careful repair after being broken a few too many times. Not impressive at all. He looked back at Tlalli as if trying to work out if she was being sarcastic or what.

Jesús, sitting on the other side of me, was also looking around the room and then at his sister. He asked her something in Spanish and she answered. It was just a few short sentences, but to my ear I thought there was something not quite Spanish about some of those words. Then he was looking around again, as if desperately trying to see something more than what was there.

I hopped up from my chair, setting my hot chocolate aside with reluctance before running to catch my grandmother before she could disappear behind her bar. But I was too late. By the time I was behind the bar, she was down in the cellar.

Had she just ditched me on purpose?

"Did you find a boat?" Loke asked, and I turned my attention back to the others around the space heater.

"We did," Michelle said.

"You'll never believe who," Jessica said.

"Simon," I said.

"How did you know?" Jessica asked.

Michelle gave her a friendly slug on the arm. "Who else would she never believe?"

"How big is the boat?" I asked. I remembered my drawing of it. It hadn't seemed that big. It usually went out with two men working on it, but was there room for many more? Would we have to ride in the fish hold?

"Not big," Jessica admitted.

Andrew set his mug aside and went back to the door to get his laptop out of his backpack. He set it on one of the tables and connected to the meeting hall's wifi.

"Simon says he can only take three of us out on the water," Michelle said. "Actually, what he said in the first place was that he wanted to go out alone, but I didn't think that was a very good idea."

"No," I said distractedly, but then looked up at her. "Why not, do you think?"

"He's so angry," Jessica said. "If we send him out alone, he's going to come back alone. If you know what I mean."

"The last thing we need is one more dead body," Michelle said, arching her eyebrow before taking a sip from her mug.

"Where is he now?" I asked.

I was asking about Simon, but it was Andrew who answered me, speaking about Adam. "He's nearly there."

"Can we reach him in time?" I asked.

"I have no idea," Andrew admitted. "The weather seems to be slowing him down. But it would slow us down too."

"Maybe this isn't worth the risk," Loke said.

"It is to me," Tlalli said. "I'm going."

"Me too," Jessica said.

"Wait," I said, holding up my hands. "There isn't enough room on the boat for all of us."

"So what, you want to draw straws or something?" Michelle asked.

"If you're going, I'm going," Andrew said, jutting out his chin in a way that dared me to argue with him.

"There isn't enough room on the boat," I said. "And no, I don't think drawing straws is the answer. This can't be random."

"Can't it?" Loke asked. I glared at him. I knew what he was thinking. To a Viking, there was nothing more worthy of trust than the luck of the draw. The gods favored the lucky because they *were* more worthy.

"Maybe we need a Plan B," I said. "Some of us can try to reach him in time on Simon's boat, but the rest of us need to find another way to tip off the police about Adam."

"I know what you're thinking," Tlalli said, crossing her arms. "I'm not staying behind."

"You know Adam better than any of us," I said. "You can tell them about the Rohypnol and his general character both."

"And I will, after we catch up to him," she said.

"This weather is getting worse by the minute," Jesús said as another blast of wind shook the walls of the meeting hall. "Is this really boating weather? Maybe Plan B is the only plan."

"Ichtaca-" Tlalli started to say. I blinked in surprise. Apparently she wasn't the only one with two names.

"No," he interrupted her. "Nothing is solved with you or anyone else at the bottom of this lake. But especially not you."

The two of them stared at each other in some sort of battle of wills I knew I was missing the context for.

But to my surprise, it was Tlalli who blinked first. "Fine. I won't go out on this little boat. I'll wait here."

"Ingrid."

I jumped at the sound of my name, not realizing that my grandmother had come back up from the cellar and was standing right behind me. "I wanted to talk to you," I whispered to her as I turned around.

"Take these," she said, pressing something into my hands. When I looked down my left hand was holding a small leather bag. On the palm of my right hand was a stack of gold disks. Not coins, though. They looked like little golden Viking shields.

"What's this?" I asked, closing my hands over the objects before anyone else could see them.

"Speed and protection," she told me.

"What are we protecting?" I asked. "Simon's boat?"

"Of course not, dear," she said to me. "That boat is much too small. But it's probably better that you're gone before he gets here. I can explain it to him better alone."

"Explain to Simon why we don't need his boat?" I asked, and she nodded. "I wished you'd explain it to me."

"You need a bigger boat," she said. "A ship, in fact. So you shall have one. This," she squeezed my left hand, "will fill the sails. You will reach the other boat in time, no worries there. And this," she squeezed my right hand, and the little disks pressed into my flesh, "will protect the ship from harm."

"But the spells of hiding," I said. "I don't know those. Aren't you coming with us?"

"Alas, no," she said. "I am, as always, chiefly needed here."

"But I can't do those spells without you," I said.

"The remnants of the spells I cast before remain. That faded magic plus this storm will hide you well enough," she said.

"It's big enough for all of us, that's true," I said. "But do even Loke or Roarr know how to sail it?"

"They know as well as any Villmarker," my grandmother said. "But they will answer to the captain, I'm sure."

"And who's the captain?" I asked. "Please don't say me."

Another gust of wind shook the hall, and the back door blew open with a bang.

Then the silhouette of a large man appeared in the doorway, and I knew the wind had only ripped the door out of his grip, not blown it open entirely.

"Are we ready?" he asked as he stepped into the light. It was Thorbjorn. An unarmed Thorbjorn, dressed like a Runde fisherman, head to toe prepared for all the wet a storm on Lake Superior could throw his way.

"I regret I won't be going," my grandmother said.

"That is a shame, but I suppose duty calls," Thorbjorn said, and she nodded. "Fine. How many of these others?"

"That's up to Ingrid, I believe," my grandmother said.

"Up to me?" I repeated. I could feel the eyes of the others on us, although we were too far away for them to hear what we were saying. There were a few whispers I took to be someone explaining who Thorbjorn was to Tlalli and Jesús.

"Of course," my grandmother said. Her chipper tone was starting to really puzzle me.

"We're talking about the Viking ship here, right?" I asked, and they both nodded. "This was dilemma enough when I thought we were going out in a modern boat. But the Viking ship? Doesn't that mean it has to just be Loke and Roarr? I mean, the rules."

My grandmother said nothing, just smiled at me as if she was waiting for me to figure something out on my own.

Thorbjorn just said, "needs must."

"What does *that* mean?" I demanded.

"Andrew, Michelle and Jessica are already very close to figuring things out," my grandmother told me. "And they wouldn't be the first."

"So I should just tell them now? To, what, get ahead of it? Spin the story?"

"Something like that," my grandmother said.

"What will the council say?" I asked.

She fluttered a hand dismissively. "They always say something. I generally leave worrying about my response until they actually say whatever it is they want to say. It's seldom as dire as you're thinking."

I looked at Thorbjorn.

"These are your friends?" he said, and I nodded. "You trust them?" I nodded again. "Then I trust them," he said. "Is there more to discuss?"

"I suppose not," I said, all too aware that time was precious. "But what about the others?"

"What others?" Thorbjorn asked.

"My friends from back home, Tlalli and Jesús," I said. He looked past me to pick them out of the small crowd behind me.

"Oh, those two?" my grandmother said with another little wave of her hand. "They already know."

"They already *know*? How is that possible? They've only been here maybe ten minutes," I said.

"Yes, they've only been here for a few minutes, but they've been to other places," she said. Then she gave me a more serious look. "They can keep secrets. Even this one. Perhaps especially this one."

"They were looking around before," I said to her. "They can see the mead hall, can't they? Even though we haven't done the spell work yet."

"She can," my grandmother said. "He... almost."

"I have so many questions," I said.

"But so little time," Thorbjorn said.

"You're right," I said. "Fine. We're all going. It doesn't feel like enough to man the ship, though."

"Hence the bag of winds," my grandmother said, tapping my left hand again. Then she crossed the room to the others. "Finish up those chocolates and run to the bathroom now if you need to. Who knows when you'll get the chance next. Then everyone gather up at the back door. I have oilskins for all of you."

"We're all going?" Jessica asked.

"Yes," I said. "Thorbjorn here has a ship that will fit all of us."

"And it's here, in Runde?" Jessica asked. "How come I've never seen a ship that size here before?"

"Who cares?" Michelle said before I could come up with an answer. "We're going to catch the bad guy. That's all that matters."

How I wished that were true. But while it was the most important thing, the highest priority thing, once we had the bad guy, everything else was going to start mattering again.

And whatever my grandmother said, I couldn't help worrying about what the Villmark council was going to say.

CHAPTER 19

*A*fter we all suited up in oilskin bib overalls and knee-length jackets and then headed out the backdoor, I admit I started to get a little less anxious and a lot more excited. I mean, I remembered just how blown away I had been the first time I had laid eyes on the Viking ship, and I had already known there was a village of descendants from the Viking Age living a stone's throw away from Runde. I could only imagine the looks that would be on my friends' faces in about ten minutes.

But that excitement didn't make it much past the end of the meeting hall's back patio before dying away again. Because the trail beyond was steep and treacherous in the best of weather. And the strengthening storm was far from the best of weather. Even I, who knew the trail well, was having some trouble climbing up it. The oilskins were blocking the wind and keeping me dry, but they were a bulky fit on me and made moving awkward.

Worst of all, the soles of my sea boots were designed for a boat's slippery deck, not a rocky trail. Aside from feeling every rock through the thin sole of my boot despite the thickness of my wool socks, I slipped and stumbled more than once on the wet path. Thorbjorn had to catch my elbow to keep me from spilling to the ground.

I looked back to see the others also employing the buddy system to get up the slope. Roarr had a steadying hand on Michelle's back, but was also looking behind them constantly to be sure that Andrew and Jessica were doing okay. Jesús and Tlalli trailed a bit behind them, going more slowly but being more sure of their steps before they took them. Loke walked alone behind all the others. Loke was wearing oilskins like the rest of us, only he had a way of making his outfit just present differently. I mean, it looked like he had his hands in his pockets as he walked, but our bibs didn't have pockets.

It was a relief to finally reach the cave behind the waterfall, ironically because despite the ever-present dampness of the air, it was drier than outside. I pushed back my sou'wester now that the rain had stopped lashing at my eyes, then stepped to one side to wait for the others to gather in the cave before continuing on down to the harbor.

"Well met, brother," Thoralv said from where he was leaning against the cave wall, the light from the bonfire around the corner dancing all around him. The leggings and tunic he wore might pass as normal modern clothes. The cloak around his shoulders would be more of a stretch. But it was too long past Halloween to explain away the assortment of weapons he was carrying.

"We're going below, to take the ship out," Thorbjorn told him as Michelle and Roarr stomped their way into the cavern. Roarr guided her to a deeper part of the cave as she too pushed back her sou'wester.

But once her hat was out of her eyes and she saw Thoralv standing there dressed like a very committed LARPer, her jaw dropped open.

"Wait a minute," she said, leaving Roarr's side to grab at my arm. "That big guy who has the ship. He's that Viking you saw your first night here!"

"Yes," I admitted. "Thorbjorn. And Thoralv here is his brother."

"I feel like I've met your fellow before, but it's like it was in a dream," she said, frowning. "But no. It was in the meeting hall, wasn't it? No, that's not what I'm remembering."

"It's all going to make more sense in a little bit," I promised her. I sensed that the more I showed my friends, the weaker the forgetting spell's hold on them became. "I think your memories will sort of click into place."

"How?" she asked.

But Jessica and Andrew were inside now, and Jessica's boots slapped loudly as she ran over to us. "This place is amazing!" she said. "I had no idea this was back here! How did I have no idea this was back here? I mean, the trail started right behind the meeting hall. We kids used to play by the river all the time when our parents were having meetings or playing bingo or whatever. We must have seen it."

"How far does it go?" Andrew asked, trying to look down the length of the cave behind Thoralv. But of course that cave took a turn, the bonfire beyond nothing more than a pattern of light on the stone walls here.

"You're not going this way, my friend," Thoralv told him. He was smiling both with his eyes and with his mouth, but that didn't disguise the fact that his words were a warning.

"There's another path we're going down," I said to Andrew. He was still trying to see what was behind Thoralv, but when I spoke he turned his gaze to me.

"You knew this was here?" he asked.

"Yes," I said.

"That's your Viking friend," he said, pointing at Thorbjorn. "I had forgotten him. How did I forget him?"

"You were supposed to," I said. "But not anymore. Bringing you all here, even though I'm not showing you everything, it changes things."

"What are you talking about?" he asked. But then Tlalli and Jesús were inside the cavern, and Tlalli's eyes were wide and wet with tears. She kept speaking something over and over, not in English but not in Spanish either.

"I see it," Jesús said to her. He started to walk towards the bonfire, but Thoralv stepped in front of him, holding a palm out in a gentle suggestion that he stop.

"Ingrid," Tlalli said, catching hold of my arm and looking imploringly into my eyes. "I have so many questions for you. I had no idea you could do this. But then, I suppose you had no idea about me either."

"No," I said, not entirely sure what she was referring to, but I could make a pretty good guess. She had seen the spells in the meeting hall, and I could see on her face that she knew from the firelight reflecting off the cave walls that the bonfire just out of her line of sight was no ordinary fire. She knew something about magic, some kind of magic, but was it anything like the magic I knew?

"We're going below now," Thorbjorn said, waving us all over to the far side of the cave, closer to the waterfall. Loke brushed past the others to lead the way, and the Runde natives adjusted their sou-westers before one by one following Loke down the path that had to be taken step by step, walking sideways, the waterfall mere inches from our noses.

"If asked, I will have to answer," Thoralv told his brother, mostly ignoring Jesús who was lifting Thoralv's cloak to get a closer look at his weapons.

"I understand," Thorbjorn said. "Nora said she will answer for all, but I would rather for now you put all the responsibility on me."

"And me," I piped in.

"No," Thorbjorn said. "Just me."

"That doesn't make any sense. I brought all these people here," I said.

"She has you there, brother," Thoralv said.

"We'll argue about later," Thorbjorn grumbled, although whether he intended to argue with his brother or with me I wasn't sure. "Time is short, and the storm is worsening."

"I will be here when you return," Thoralv said with a little bow.

Thorbjorn had to catch Jesús by the shoulder and steer him away. Tlalli lingered for a moment as if basking in the reflected light from the fire, but when I brushed my hand against her arm, she moved to follow me on her own.

"It's been so long," she said. "How large of a place have you pock-eted off? Of course, I mean that your family pocketed off. Your ancestors. I gather you didn't know this place existed until you moved up here, since you never visited as a child."

"I was here when I was very young," I said. "But I didn't come back even to visit, and I forgot all about it. Wait a minute, just where did you and Jesús used to go when you were kids? He said Mexico City. To visit your mother and your grandmother."

"That *is* true," Tlalli said. We had to stop talking for a moment as the path reached its narrowest point, just as it bent around an outcropping of rock. But then the path widened once more, diving deep into the hill before curving down to the harbor below, and we were able to walk side by side again.

"There is a place like this in Mexico City?" I asked.

"There was," Tlalli said, brushing a tear from the corner of one eye. "I lost it."

"You lost it?" I asked.

"Jesús probably told you my mother is dead, but we don't actually know if that's true," she said. "We went to visit her one summer, like we did all the times before, but when we got there, I couldn't find the way in. It was just... gone. Something happened. I think my mother is trapped on the other side, but until I find a way to get back to her, I'll never know for sure. But tell me about this place."

"An ancestor of mine created it to hide her people from enemies who were pursuing them. The first settlers here were from an island off the coast of what's now Norway. They lived in the Viking Age, before there was a Norway, and they've been here ever since. They're not really Vikings now. That was a raiding cultural activity they never did here. They've been fishermen and farmers ever since, but they descended from Vikings," I said.

"My mother's home was similar, I think," Tlalli said. "Our ancestor pocketed away one of the manmade islands of México-Tenochtitlán, to hide us from the conquistadores. In this world, the entrance looked like the courtyard behind some old buildings in the center of the city. But on the other side, they've got the whole lake to themselves. Some of their ways are like the old ways, but others are different. Like what you said about your Viking ancestors no longer being able to raid like

Vikings. Without surrounding communities, a lot changed for my people too. But I was a child when I visited there, I was never allowed to see what was beyond the shores of the lake."

"There are dangers here as well, if you go too deep," I said.

"I have so many questions for you," Tlalli said. "So much I need to understand. I was too young when I lost my mother, I hadn't learned nearly enough, and my grandmother never had any interest in any of it. I love her, but she can't help me with this. She left that place to be a modern girl decades ago and never looked back."

"My grandmother might be more help than me," I admitted. "But I know she'll help all she can."

Then we emerged on the beach, and I couldn't help showing off one of the few spells I actually knew, conjuring a ball of light to illuminate the entire harbor. The others were still working their way around the shore, using their cellphones as flashlights, but they all cried out in oohs and ahs as my light grew from a little ball on my palm to a starburst that hung like a firework display frozen in time over the mast of the Viking ship.

"Come on," I said to Tlalli, "let's catch up."

She nodded, and we jogged over the sand to where the others were clamoring over the side of the Viking ship.

Where Nilda and Kara were waiting for us.

"Those weren't costumes," Andrew said when he saw them. Even though they were in the same oilskins the rest of us were wearing, I could see why he would immediately draw that conclusion. No matter what they were wearing, when they stood like that, so tall and broad-shouldered, there was no hiding that they had the spirits of valkyries if not the actual winged horses.

"Like we were going to let you confront Gullveig's killer without us," Kara said to me.

"Of course not," I said. "Did Thorbjorn send for you?"

"No, that was me," Loke said as he climbed over the side. "Your grandmother summoned her favorite boy, but I called Nilda and Kara myself."

"Thanks," I said.

"The oars are stowed and we'll leave them that way, but the rowing benches are still the safest places to sit," Thorbjorn said. "One to a bench, stay close to the center of the ship and away from the waves. But not you," he said, catching me by the shoulders before I could sit on the bench behind Andrew.

"Where do you want me?" I asked. He didn't answer, just walked me to the back of the ship to where my grandmother's little stool sat alone.

"We can't get out of here until you part the waters," he reminded me.

"Of course," I said, but my mouth had gone suddenly dry. I had gotten the ship through the waterfall once before, when my grandmother had been too tired to finish the spell herself, but it still felt a lot like a fluke to me. Opening the bag of winds? I was sure I could handle that. But I had to get us out of the harbor first.

"Shields!" I said, digging into my jacket pocket for the gold disks. "Put these all around the outside of the ship."

Thorbjorn took them from me, then passed them out to the others. Everyone leaned over the side of the ship at the end of their bench and pressed the disk into the hull, then resumed their seats closer to the center of the ship.

I took out my sketchbook and settled it on my lap. It was awkward, the oilskin jacket was so bulky. Hopefully, it was the intent that mattered and not the artistic execution, because my arm was only capable of moving in the broadest of strokes.

I closed my eyes, pencil in hand but not touching the page yet. I could hear the storm even over the sound of the falling water, the wind shrieking then moaning before building up to another shriek. I didn't know who usually wore the oilskins I was swaddled in, but the oily smell of the exterior was overwhelmed by the mildewy smell coming from the softer lining.

Mildew, but also old sweat.

I focused on the sweat smell, imagining the fisherman who had exuded that sweat so many years ago, perhaps in a storm much like this one. They had made it through all right, or else the clothes I was wearing would've ended up on the bottom of the lake.

I put my pencil tip down on the page and started to draw the outline of the ship, the shields all around that protected us from the wind and rain as much as from the spears and arrows of humans.

I drew us all huddled on the benches in our over-sized jackets with the long backs of our sou-westers obscuring our identities. But I knew each shape that I drew. I knew Loke's lanky frame, Thorbjorn's hulk, Andrew's more hidden strength.

Only when I had each of us drawn on the boat did I start drawing in the waterfall before us in great swooping strokes. It curved away from the center, like a part in a stage curtain, just large enough to let the ship pass through.

Then, still without opening my eyes, I reached into my lefthand pocket and took out the bag of winds. I set it on my palm facing the mast before me.

I loosened the strings and opened the mouth of the bag, and the ship beneath me shot off like a rocket.

CHAPTER 20

*A*ll I could do was hold on. It was absolutely terrifying. I could feel the hull of the ship skipping over the waves of the river.

Then we reached the lake, and the skipping started to feel a lot more like one of those jets that simulates free fall by going straight up and down. You know the one I mean? The Vomit Comet.

I gripped the stool beneath me, but then I remembered that wasn't exactly attached to the ship. It was just sitting on the deck like I was sitting by a campfire, not bolted down in any way.

I forced myself to take a deep breath and keep the panic at bay. But I only needed to get a little calmer before I could feel the protective magic from those shields all around us. They surrounded all of us in a golden light, and I knew nothing was going to hurt us while we were on that ship.

I opened my eyes. I saw my sketchbook laying on the deck at my feet, pages rustling in the wind, and bent over to pick it up and tuck it back away inside my messenger bag under my jacket. The pencil had disappeared, but I had plenty of others.

I looked up to see Andrew making his way back to me one careful step at a time. There was nothing to hold on to, no railing or even the back of any chairs, just the benches that were below the height of his knees. And he had his laptop open in one hand. But he was managing it all right, riding with the motion of the ship like he'd been doing this forever.

"Ingrid," he said, coming around to stand beside me and set the laptop on my knees. "My cellphone is losing bars and the hot spot keeps dropping, but here's the last image."

I looked at the map on the screen. The icon that was labeled *Fortune's Fool* was most of the way from Isle Royale to Thunder Bay. "The name. He sent his information to the monitoring service?"

"Yes," Andrew said. "He must be getting nervous, being out alone in this sudden burst of bad weather. But he's moving towards shore."

"Is he in Canadian waters already?" I asked.

"I don't know," he said.

"It doesn't matter," Thorbjorn said from where he had come around behind me to also look at the screen. "We will bring him home. He will be arrested here, not in Canada."

"Can we do that?" Andrew asked.

"Of course," Thorbjorn said.

"I mean legally?" Andrew said. Thorbjorn just scoffed, then straightened up to scan the waters before us.

The waters in question being everywhere. The rolling waves, the wind that scattered the breaking tops of those waves, the never-ending sheets of rain. It was all water and nothing but water.

But none of it was touching us on the deck of the ship. We could feel wind, but only from our great speed, not from the storm itself, and that wind carried no rain. If I squinted just right, I could see the golden light that kept it all at bay. But without squinting, it just looked like we were dodging all the drops in some improbable dance.

"How fast are we going, do you think?" I asked.

"Fast enough," Thorbjorn said. "We'll be there soon."

Andrew snapped his laptop closed then tucked it away in his backpack, carefully drawing the closures tight, although they were not remotely waterproof. Then he shifted, still in a squat but now looking up at me. "You're doing this? All this?" he asked. There was warmth in his dark blue eyes, a degree of admiration I just knew I didn't deserve.

"Well, the Villmarkers built the ship themselves," I said. "I don't know where my grandmother got the bag of winds or the protective shields from. It feels like very old magic to me. I just opened the bag, and the old magic took over. And you all put the shields up."

"And when the waterfall parted like a curtain to let us out of the hidden harbor?" he asked, the intensity in his eyes still making me squirm.

"Yeah, that was me," I admitted. "My grandmother has been teaching me magic. It runs in my family, I guess. But I've missed out on years of instruction. I'm really not very good at any of this yet."

"So you really have been epically busy," he said.

"What, you thought I was just making that up?" I asked.

He flushed. "Well, I've seen your art," he said, not meeting my eyes. "It's good! But I've also seen you draw, and I know how long it takes you to finish something. And I've seen how much you've done."

"How have you seen all that?" I demanded.

He flushed a darker red. "Sometimes I come by, and you're busy. I mean, not there. And your grandmother gives me coffee, foists some baked goods on me, and shows me what you've been working on. I assumed she told you."

"No," I said. "Not a word. How often have you been stopping by?"

He didn't say anything, but I had a feeling the answer was something close to "every day."

"So you figured with how long it takes me to finish a drawing and how many drawings you saw, you could calculate how much time I was spending on my art?" I asked. "That's a lot of math."

"Well," he said, but had no followup. He could tell I was annoyed. But I didn't like the feeling that I had been failing an evaluation I didn't even know I was undergoing.

"And I was coming up several hours a day short," I said. "Which is true. But it's not like it was ever any of your business if I wasted my time. Not that I did! Most of my time has gone to my new studies. Magic and history and culture and an entire language that is spoken nowhere else in the world."

"But your grandmother never told you when I stopped by?" he asked. "Ever?"

"No," I said. "It must have slipped her mind."

But just like that, my anger had deflated. Why *hadn't* my grandmother told me about all these little visits? At the very least, so I could make them stop? Had it really slipped her mind?

That was a chilling thought. I decided to go back to the paranoia that my grandmother was trying to micromanage my social life. That was easier to deal with.

Tlalli was moving from bench to bench towards us. I couldn't blame her for not trusting herself to stand or walk like Andrew and Thorbjorn were doing. I had no plans to get up from my stool myself. She stopped at the last of the benches and sat backwards to lean forward over her knees and say to me, "this is amazing!"

"I didn't do much," I said. Her admiration was even harder to accept than Andrew's. "My grandmother had the bag of winds and the shields."

"I've seen things like the shields before. Gold has a very strong affinity for magic," she said. "But nothing like that bag. And the magic you invoked to open the waterfall! I tried to follow the flow of the spell but I couldn't quite catch it."

"Maybe because it's not really a spell," I said. I dug my sketchbook back out of the bag under my jacket, then showed her the last drawing. "I don't say words or make hand gestures or anything. I just draw."

Tlalli took the sketchbook from me and examined the page, running her fingertips over the penciled markings. "Does you grandmother draw as well?"

"Not that I know of," I said.

"Look!" Andrew said, straightening up to point to something off the righthand side of the ship. "That's Isle Royale!"

"So we're nearly there," I said. "That *was* fast."

"Do we think he's alone on this ship of his?" Thorbjorn asked me. His eyes were still staring straight ahead of us into the storm, watching for the first sign of the yacht.

"Yes, that's what the guard at the marina said," Tlalli said.

"I saw a picture of his yacht at his house," I said. "It's not big. He can probably crew it himself, and it looks like he mainly used it to bring about a dozen people out on the water for parties."

"Is he armed?" Thorbjorn asked.

"That I don't know," I said. I looked at Tlalli, who shrugged. "We didn't see any sign of guns in his house, but we were only in the front hall and his bedroom. I suppose we'd have to assume at least a flare gun, knives from the galley, maybe more."

Thorbjorn nodded, then looked to Nilda and Kara, who were turned in their seats, watching us from the front row of benches. He raised a fist, and they turned to start digging in the chests under the bench seats. Within seconds, they were fully armed with axes, swords, knives and spears.

"Is that really going to be necessary?" I asked.

"Better safe than sorry," Thorbjorn said. "Loke, arm up!" he yelled. Loke turned on his bench to look back at us. He made a little motion with his arm and suddenly had a knife balanced by the tip of its blade on one thumb. Then he repeated the motion, and it was gone again.

"I guess he thinks that will be enough," I said. Then I heard Andrew suck in a breath. "What is it?"

"Luke. There's something about him. Is he part of all this? But I've known him forever."

"His name is Loke," I said. "He's a Villmarker, like Thorbjorn and Roarr. But he feels just as at home in Runde. So your memories of him aren't warped by the magic that protects Villmark. I assume."

"Ship!" Thorbjorn yelled, pointing ahead of us. It took a moment for me to be sure of what I was seeing. At first it was just a blur of light through the rain, but then the light became lights, and those lights outlined the shape of a yacht. It was all sleek lines, the windows hidden behind the sides of the deck. If anyone was on board, we saw no sign of them.

"Pack up! We're leaving nothing behind!" Thorbjorn said as he marched down the center of the ship to stand at the prow. I put my sketchbook away again, then fastened up my oilskin jacket. If I fell overboard, it was all going to get soaked, but at least I could protect it from the rain and blowing lake water.

"We'll go first and make sure the deck is clear," Nilda said. "When we give the signal, the rest of you follow."

Kara had something like a harpoon gun in her hands and when our ship was close enough, she fired it into the side of the yacht. It pierced the sleek ivory body of the boat, almost as upsetting a sight as if she had speared a whale. The owner might be a loathsome individual, but it was still a really nice boat.

Thorbjorn stepped beside Kara to catch onto the line and help her draw the Viking ship up tight against the yacht's side. Then she and Nilda scaled up the side of the yacht, disappearing over the railing above us.

"Second group?" Roarr asked, standing ready beside Loke. He was armed up like Nilda and Kara, with knives in his belt and a sword and spear across his back, but his hands were free.

"Not yet," Thorbjorn said. Then Kara and Nilda's faces appeared over the rail, dropping a rope ladder and waving for us to climb up to them.

"Help them hold the deck in case anyone comes up from below," he said to Roarr and Loke. "You two up next," he said to Jesús and Tlalli. "Then you two," he said to Michelle and Jessica. They nodded, and he looked past them to Andrew and I. "You two will follow them. I'll go last."

I watched Loke and Roarr scaling the side of the yacht. The first rungs of the ladder were fairly easy, although the rocking of the two ships over the waves was both erratic and unrelenting. Then they emerged from the Viking ship's protective barrier and were out in the storm. I could see it hit them both. It was like I could feel the breath being sucked from their bodies.

"This is going to be fun," Andrew said as he adjust the chin strap of his sou-wester. Like me, he had put his backpack on under his oilskin jacket, making him look like a mutant turtle in disguise as an ordinary pizza customer on a very rainy day.

Roarr and Loke pulled themselves over the rail. I just caught a glimpse of Roarr drawing his sword before he moved out of sight. Then Tlalli and Jesús were climbing up the rope ladder.

"When you get to the top, find some cover and wait," Thorbjorn said to Michelle and Jessica. "Once we know it's just the one guy and we've captured him, we can let our guard down, but not before."

They both nodded. There was something in the sternness of their eyes, in the strength of their body language, that reminded me of the Valkyrie look Kara and Nilda always had. Perhaps they also descended from warriors. One by one Thorbjorn boosted them as far as he could lift them, and they too started climbing the ladder.

"Should I have a weapon?" Andrew asked.

"Can you use one?" Thorbjorn asked.

"It seems pretty self-explanatory," Andrew said, looking at the axe on Thorbjorn's belt.

"You'll be fine without one," Thorbjorn said, resting a hand on Andrew's shoulder. I could imagine what he was thinking, weapons in inexperienced hands swinging wildly in the narrow confines of a yacht meant for intimate parties, but he didn't let a bit of it show. Instead, he let Andrew climb up on the prow of the ship and reach for the ladder. He didn't offer him a boost, but he did keep his hands near in case Andrew should start to topple over.

But he didn't. He caught the bottom of the ladder on the first try and pulled himself up the side of the yacht.

"Your turn," Thorbjorn said to me. I nodded, putting my booted foot into his interlaced hands.

He lifted me up into the air like I weighed nothing, but my amazement at that was only a momentary flash before I realized I had made a mistake.

The ship behind me was falling apart. The moment my bottom foot had left the deck, I felt it start to happen. Even though the shields were still stationed all around the hull, I had taken the magic powering them with me. The instant I was no longer in contact with the ship, the waves started bashing it against the side of the yacht.

"Thorbjorn!" I shrieked into the wind. I could feel his hands on my ankle, and my throat tightened with fear. At any moment, the only thing keeping us both on the side of the yacht was going to be my grip on the rope ladder. And he was heavy.

We were never going to make it. I could feel my fingers slipping on the wet rope already.

But Thorbjorn didn't drag me down. He leapt off the deck of the Viking ship and jumped past me, grasping the same rung of the ladder as I hung from.

I looked back down at the ship and felt my heart break. The waves were bashing it against the side of the yacht over and over again, and the boards were starting to break like kindling. This was so much worse than watching Kara spear the side of the yacht.

It was more than a ship; it was a living, breathing work of art. And I had just killed it.

"No!" Thorbjorn yelled at me, as if he could sense my fingers letting go of the ladder before it even quite happened. He snaked an arm around me and held me fast against his side.

"I can save it if I go back," I said.

"We can build another," he said. "Let it go."

I squirmed, but it was pretty obvious that trying to break free from his hold was never going to happen. And the deck below us was already half underwater. Then the rope holding the ship against the side of the yacht snapped. The ship rolled back with the next wave, then a little further back with the wave after that.

The third wave caught it crossways, rolling it over on its side. By the fourth wave, it was gone.

I don't know how I got up that ladder. I suspect Thorbjorn carried me as much as I climbed. The rain in my eyes was too blinding to see what was happening. Then hands reached out to pull me over the railing and I sat down hard on the deck, mostly out of the wind.

It wasn't rain in my eyes. It was tears.

Thorbjorn landed more gracefully on the deck beside me, then crouched down to gather me up in his arms.

"I know," he said. "I know. The next one won't be the same. Not without Solvi."

"I'm being silly," I said, wiping at my eyes. "It's just, it deserved a better end."

"It brought us here," he said. Then added with a twinkle in his eye, "you can say it died in battle. There's no better end than that."

That got a laugh out of me. Not a big one, but still it eased some of the tightness around my heart.

We both turned at the sound of boots running across the deck to where we stood by the rail.

"There you are," Andrew said, his eyes moving between us. They didn't have to move far; we were standing very close. I took half a step back away from Thorbjorn and swiped the last of the tears from my face. "You better come quick," Andrew said.

"What is it?" Thorbjorn asked, his hand on the handle of his axe.

"We found Adam," Andrew said. "He isn't at the helm like he ought to be. He's below. And the only cool head down there with him is Loke."

That was not good.

"Lead the way," Thorbjorn said grimly.

CHAPTER 21

*I*t wasn't easy moving around on that yacht. The Viking ship had been hard enough, but it had been taking the waves head-on and magically propelling through them. Not only was there no magic aiding us now, there wasn't even anyone at the wheel. Now we were at the mercy of every errant wave, bucking and rolling this way and that.

At least it wasn't far to the door that led below decks, and then we were out of the lashing cold rain. I pushed back my sou'wester to drain the water from its rolled-up brim and get it out of my eyes, but then nearly fell through an open doorway to my left as the yacht climbed a wave then slid down the back of it sideways.

"Can you captain this vessel?" Thorbjorn asked Andrew. They had both lunged to catch me before I fell, and for a moment they each had a hold of one of my arms. Then I was standing between them, but Thorbjorn behind me had no trouble keeping eye contact with Andrew in front of me. I wasn't exactly short, I was on the tall side of average in height, but in that moment it was like I wasn't even there.

"I don't think so," Andrew said to Thorbjorn. "But I'll go up and look. At the very least, I can put out a distress call."

"Do it," Thorbjorn said.

167

"Wait, Adam?" I said as Andrew started to run up the hallway. He looked back towards me but didn't quite meet my eyes. Well, he was in a hurry to keep us from all getting dumped in the lake if the yacht turned over. Which was clearly a good possibility.

"They're all in that room there," he said, pointing to his right as he ran to the end of the hall and up a set of stairs so steep it was nearly a ladder. Then he was gone, and Thorbjorn and I headed for the closed door he had pointed to.

We could hear voices, angry voices, and someone sobbing in terror. That one wasn't hard to guess, even before we pushed the door open to find a dark-haired young man cowering in a chair, Nilda and Kara both leaning over him with long knives drawn.

I hadn't gotten a good look at Adam in that photo in his room, just a general sense of a rich kid who dressed well but not flashy. He was dressed much the same now, his fashion sense apparently confined to knowing which labels were the "right" labels. And his dark hair was cut in that dual-purpose style where he could slick it back for an office look or let it flop over his forehead like a K-Pop star for parties.

But at the moment all of that was subtext, because his designer clothes were wrinkled and stained as if he had been wearing the same outfit for days. Maybe even since Gullveig had died. And that floppy hair was hanging limply over his bloodshot eyes.

He looked like he'd been having an awful time even before two Norse women had shown up to threaten him with knives.

"Stand down," Thorbjorn said to the two of them in his growliest voice.

"Oh, thank you," Adam said when Nilda and Kara stepped back. But they didn't put the knives away, and the look of grateful relief that had washed over his face immediately shifted back to trepidation. He looked up at Thorbjorn expectantly but then his brows drew together in confusion when Thorbjorn merely shut the door behind us then stood in front of it with arms crossed like the bouncer outside of a VIP room.

I looked around the cabin. It was cozy like a family space, with couches built into the curve of the hull all along one wall, an entertainment center on the wall opposite. There was a wet bar on my left and bookshelves on my right. Adam had taken a seat at a pull-down desk, all the cubbies with little panels to keep the contents safe in rough weather. Rather like what we were in now. There was a family portrait over the desk, as well as a large drawing of Lake Superior. Not a proper chart, more art than map.

All that makes the space sound bigger than it was. I'm sure it was great for a family of four, particularly if half that family were kids. But with ten of us piled up on those couches and leaning against every shelf and table, it was a bit claustrophobic.

So I had to squeeze past some shoulders and elbows when I stepped forward to stand right in front of where Adam cowered in the desk chair. Adam's eyes finally jumped from Thorbjorn to me. He didn't seem to quite be able to focus on me. Then I smelled alcohol in the room and looked around to see a spilled bottle on the floor. Rum. It looked like most of the bottle was soaking the carpet, but there were other empty bottles tossed in one corner.

Great. It looked like I was going to be racing against time to get answers out of him before he passed out entirely. I hadn't anticipated that wrinkle.

"You're Adam Taylor?" I said.

"Who's asking?" he shot back. His tone was sufficiently aggressive, but the swallowing thing he did afterward spoke more of nerves. He was going for bluster to hide his fear, but he was failing.

"You already know who we are," Kara said darkly.

"No, I don't," he insisted. "You just said friends of Gullveig, but the only friend of hers I knew was Lisa. And Lisa is dead!"

"We should ask him about that too," Jessica hissed from where she was sitting pressed up against Michelle on the couch.

"No," Roarr said. He started to say more, but I shot him a furious glare and he sat back down, his eyes on the hands twisting together in his lap.

"Who *are* you people?" Adam asked and gulped again.

"You met Gullveig at Lisa's memorial service, correct?" I asked.

"Look, what you need to understand is-" he started to say, when Nilda leaned forward and pricked his thigh with the tip of her knife.

"Nilda!" I gasped.

"Sorry," she said in the least apologetic tone ever.

"Stick to yes or no," Kara said to Adam. "Answer her questions and only her questions. Is that clear?"

His eyes were on her knife, but the focus had gone all fixated and I was worried he was about to pass out right then and there. Then the yacht made another sickening roll, and it seemed more likely he would vomit first.

I had never actually seen anyone turn green before. I always thought that only happened in cartoons. But this was no time for sympathy.

"You met Gullveig at Lisa's memorial service, correct?" I said again.

"Yes! Yes!" he said from behind the hand pressed to his mouth. He swallowed, then shakily dropped his hand. "I had seen her around before that, at parties, but I never met her until that day. Is that answer enough for you?"

Thorbjorn made a growling sound that was almost subaudible, rumbling through the room like a stereo set to all bass, no treble.

"Then what happened?" I asked. "The two of you made a date?"

"No, not at first," he said. "She was playing it coy."

"Gullveig didn't play," Nilda said.

"Didn't she?" Adam asked, as if that didn't make any sense to him. Then he started to spiral, babbling nonsense. "Did she? Was she?"

I snapped my fingers in front of his face to get his attention focused back on me. "What happened at the service? She agreed to meet you later?"

"No, but she said some things," he mumbled. "I gathered that she had Lisa's cellphone. I don't know why, but she had it and it still worked, so I started texting her."

"She knew it was you?" I asked.

"Of course she did," he said. "I mean, she was coy. Or whatever." He glanced nervously at Nilda, then at Kara, who were both watching him through narrowed eyes, knives at the ready. "It took a few weeks to even get her to agree to meet."

"Where did she meet you?" I asked. "If she was in Runde and you were in Duluth. Did you pick her up here?"

"No, she was weird about that," he said. "She wouldn't go down there, I couldn't come up here, halfway between wouldn't do either. It was a lot of work." He started to grin despite himself.

"I bet," Loke said drily. Adam glanced his way as if they were going to share that knowing grin, but when his eyes met Loke's at their flintiest, he dropped both his gaze and the annoying little smirk.

"So what happened?" I asked. "We know you saw her again."

"Yeah, I did," he admitted, shooting defiant looks at me then Loke then Thorbjorn. But the defiance melted when he locked eyes with Nilda again.

"We know this yacht was offshore near Runde on the night she died," I said.

"How do you know that?" he asked, then rubbed at his forehead. "Look, I don't have to answer your questions. I *shouldn't* answer your questions. We get ashore and I'll call my dad's lawyers and then we can see about your questions."

"I think you might be misjudging the situation," Loke said.

"How?" Adam asked.

Loke held up a finger as if commanding us all to wait for something. Then two waves rocked the yacht at once, tossing us up then down again with the sickening lurch of a rollercoaster ride. "First of all, there's that."

"And then there're the knives, right?" Adam said with a bark of a laugh. "Do you really think you'll get ashore alive without my help? Can any of you steer this craft?"

"Can *you*?" I asked. "How much have you been drinking?"

"Not enough," he said, looking at the spilled rum with something like regret. Maybe he had spilled more than one of the other bottles. Maybe it wasn't as bad as I feared. But from the look of his pupils, he was over any legal limit for boating.

"I want him to admit what he did," Nilda said. "I want to hear him say it!"

"She swam out to me!" Adam said. "I thought it was all a joke, that I'd sail up to Runde and just sit around all day while she laughed herself crazy from the shore. But I did it anyway, and sure enough, just before sunset she swam right up to the side of the yacht and climbed over the rail."

"Do you have any idea how cold that water is?" I asked.

"She was wearing a wetsuit," he said. "Look in that cabinet. It's still there."

He pointed to a door behind Kara. She turned to open it, then showed us all what was inside. A wetsuit, face mask with snorkel, and flippers.

"Would this be warm enough?" I asked.

"Could be," Kara said as she lowered her head to sniff at the suit. "I just smell lake water, not Gullveig."

"She washed ashore with clothes on," Jessica pointed out.

"Oh, she had clothes on underneath it," Adam said. "She was like a lady James Bond. One minute she was dripping on my deck in that wetsuit, the next minute she'd unzipped out of all of that and her hair was perfect, and she was wearing jeans and a top. Blouse. Whatever. Then she opened this waterproof bag she had with her and took out a sweater and a pair of flats. It was like magic."

Michelle stifled a laugh that felt more nervous reaction than genuine humor, and I ignored it.

"It sounds like a magical date indeed," I said. "You had dinner ready on the deck, I assume? Under some heaters? Or maybe in the galley down here. It's pretty snug here."

"I did have dinner waiting down here," he said. "We had roast chicken and new potatoes in a white wine sauce."

"You cook?" I asked.

"No, I brought it from a place down in Duluth," he said.

"Then what?" Nilda asked.

"Then I put it in the oven on the Keep Warm setting until I got here," he said.

"Not what she meant," I said.

"Oh. Well, *then* we went back up on the deck to drink champagne and watch the sunset."

"And then what?" Nilda asked again.

Adam risked shooting her an annoyed glance. "Then nothing. She left."

"Without her wetsuit?" I said, and Kara thrust the suit towards him in case he had forgotten it.

"She left in a hurry," he said. "Look, see this here?" He turned his face, sweeping his hair back with one hand and leaning a little further into the light. Then I saw that his left cheek was a little swollen and discolored, a bruise only partly healed.

"She did that?" Nilda asked.

"She punched me and jumped overboard," he said, throwing up his hands. "She *chose* to do that. It's not my fault."

"You didn't throw out a life preserver or anything?" I asked.

"Why? She made a beeline for the shore, and she swam like an Olympic champion. By the time I could get to a life preserver, she'd be on shore. What would be the point?" he asked.

"You watched her all the way to shore?" I asked. "You saw her get out of the water? You knew she was okay before you left?"

"Well, no," he said, rubbing at his cheek and flinching slightly. "She had just slugged me. I was angry. I could see she was fine, but I wasn't sticking around. I went home."

"But today you got back in this yacht and tried to run away," I said. "If you thought she was safe, why did you do that?"

"I read the news," he said.

"The news didn't run her picture, or even her name," I said.

"Well, who else could it have been?" he asked.

I heard the sound of distant shouting and turned to give Thorbjorn a questioning look.

"Andrew," he said. "We need this fellow manning the wheel, soonish."

"I'll get us ashore," Adam said. He started to push up from the chair, but froze when both Nilda and Kara leaned in on him. "I told you what happened! The last time I saw her, she was still alive. Whatever happened after that has nothing to do with me! Now, I'm not saying another word until we're safely ashore."

"And you safely have your lawyers," Jessica said with a glower.

"I'm entitled to lawyers," he said.

"Your story skipped over something," I said. "Romantic dinner, romantic sunset viewing, then Gullveig out of nowhere slugs you and swims away?"

"It must've been something I said," he said with a failed attempt at a charming grin.

"Or something you did," I said.

"I never laid a hand on her," he said.

"Not that you can prove that," Michelle said, and he grinned again and shrugged.

"We have proof," I said.

He looked up at me, startled. His eyes were starting to focus better. That was something.

"Proof I never touched her?" he asked like it was a dare.

"Proof of what you did," I said.

"You don't have any proof," he said, looking me over as if wondering what was in my pockets.

"Not on me," I said. "But the police know there was a date rape drug in her system when she was found. And I'm betting it's going to be a perfect match to what was prescribed to you. You know, for insomnia."

His eyes narrowed and I could see his hands closing into fists, but I didn't step back. He'd have to be a real fool to try anything.

"That doesn't prove anything," he said. "She came out here to see me. We had dinner together. That Rohypnol is in my system too, if they check. My lawyers won't have too much trouble proving we did it together. Consensually. It happens. You have nothing. Call it a death by misadventure or whatever, but not a murder."

"But it was murder," Nilda said.

"She was alive when she left here," he said again.

Nilda stepped up to lean over him in his chair. "She could've made it to shore. Even in the cold, she could've done it. Even in the dark. Even after the wine, she could've done it. But not with whatever you gave her. Not with how much you gave her. That was the one thing that makes this murder and not..." she blinked back tears before angrily spitting out the final word, "misadventure!"

"We also have a lot of character witnesses who will speak against you," Tlalli said, pushing back her hat as she sat forward on the couch. Adam looked over at her, then blanched. Apparently he had missed seeing her before, and his mind was boggling trying to connect her to Gullveig and the rest of us. "Shall I name all the names? There are many. Your lawyers can't pay them all off. Not now that someone has died. They'll talk. To save others, they will."

I heard Andrew shouting again, but his words were too muffled to be understood. Still, he sounded even more urgent than before.

"We need him upstairs, I think," I said.

"Why would I help any of you?" Adam demanded.

"You want a cold watery grave?" I asked him.

"I want my lawyers," he said, lifting his chin defiantly.

"And you'll have them," I said. "The minute we're back on American soil. You have my word."

"I trust you," he said, pointing a finger at me with a look on his face like I should be flattered.

"Thorbjorn, take him to Andrew," I said, stepping aside to let Adam past. I really, really didn't want him to brush up against me. Not even with a layer of oilskin between us.

"Ingrid," Roarr started to say, but I held up my hand.

"I meant what I said to him," I told Roarr, and I realized I was using my volva voice again. This magic thing was getting easier in random ways. Roarr nodded, but his shoulders were slumped in defeat. Nilda and Kara didn't look too pleased either, and Tlalli was frowning as well. "I meant what I said to him, exactly, those words. I think you'll find that gives us a little room. But we really do have to get to shore first."

"But where will that be? Canada?" Jessica asked.

"Yes, but not in town. Not where there'd be authorities to interfere.

No, I'm guessing he'll take us right there." I pointed to the map that hung on the wall just behind the chair where Adam had been sitting. It was gorgeous, hand-drawn. The family's home just north of Duluth was lovingly rendered, as if it were an important castle protecting that shoreline.

And in the north, on Thunder Bay, was another lovingly rendered building on the shore of the lake. The family's summer cabin.

CHAPTER 22

I felt a rumbling under my feet and realized that Adam had turned on the engines.

If only I knew how good of a boatman he was. Or how badly he wanted to get us all to safety.

"Isn't there something more we can do besides wait down here?" Jessica asked, hugging herself tightly. I saw that she and Michelle both had found life vests somewhere on the yacht and put them on over their oilskins. But as cold as the water was, staying afloat wasn't going to be enough to keep any of us alive.

"I can try to help," I said, pulling off my jacket before sitting down in the chair that Adam had just left. I spun around to face the desk and looked up at the map. Then I took my sketchbook out of my bag and started drawing.

I hadn't gotten a very good look at the yacht when we'd come aboard, not in the storm and the chaos of our sinking ship. I knew the details I was sketching weren't even from memory. I was drawing a generic yacht, a shape that surely lacked specificity. As an artist, I hated the shortcuts I was taking.

As a witch, I wasn't sure this was going to be remotely good enough for my magic.

But I did have something else to focus on: the image of the cabin on the shore from the map in front of me. I stared at the details so lovingly rendered there and recreated them on the paper under my hands. It was a home, a family home. That was stronger magic than this yacht, a mere display of wealth that hadn't even contained a family in years.

I felt hands resting on my shoulders. I didn't look up, didn't stop sketching, but I felt Tlalli's energy around me. The sounds of the storm faded away, the feel of the engines rumbling under my feet became some distant thing from the work of my hands.

As I directed all my attention on getting us safely to that home on the lake, Tlalli's energy kept expanding, blanketing the yacht much as the golden shields had covered our ship in golden light. The effect was lighter, and the size of the yacht stretched out whatever she fed into the spell until it was almost too sparse to be felt.

But I knew she was protecting us. For now. The storm behind us in the heart of the lake was growing stronger by the minute. My ears felt like they were about to explode.

"We're nearly there," Roarr said from the doorway, and I jumped, my pencil skittering across the page. "Sorry. It's just, Thorbjorn wants everyone ready to get on the boats the minute we get as close to shore as this yacht will go. Apparently Adam is going to drop anchor, but we're going to have to get into inflatable boats to get ashore. There's no dock here."

"Great," Michelle said. "We're going to be soaked."

"There's food and a fire at the house, so we'll be warm and dry soon enough," Roarr said. "Come on, we have to get up on the deck."

I put my things away and Tlalli helped me back into my jacket. Then we all tromped up the steps, back out into the wind. The waves were smaller than they had been out on the lake, but the rain was turning to stinging snow.

We followed Roarr to the front of the boat where Andrew and Thorbjorn were already lowering the boats down to the water. I looked around but could see no sign of the shore through the blowing snow.

"It's not far," Andrew said close to my ear. I nodded, tucking my chin deeper behind the collar of my jacket. The sky was darkening, both from the deepening storm and from the sun setting in the west somewhere behind all those clouds. And that growing darkness was bringing a bone-deep cold with it.

"We're set," Adam said as he emerged from the cabin. Some of the drunk look had left his eyes, but at the same time it looked like his epic hangover was just roaring to life. I didn't envy him, about to get on an inflatable boat to ride the churning waves to shore. "The beaching spot is that way. Can you see it?" he asked, pointing through the snow-filled wind.

Thorbjorn nodded, then started hustling us towards the rope ladders. He and Roarr went down first, one to each boat. Andrew and Loke manned the tops of the ladders, helping the rest of us get over the rail and climb down to the boats.

They looked so flimsy on the riotous water.

I found myself sitting with my back to the wall of the boat, tucked up tight inside my jacket with my hood pulled down low. The snow cut like ice, and it was impossible to see through everything blowing through the air. I wasn't even sure who else was on the same boat with me.

But I knew the minute we broke away from the yacht. Someone pressed an oar into my hands, and I turned to row with all the strength I had.

Michelle was right. We all got soaked despite our oilskins before we'd made more than three strokes with our oars.

Then I felt the pressure on my ears ramp up so painfully I had to stop rowing and just clutch my oar and focus on my breathing until it passed.

But it wasn't passing. I could feel something behind me, out in the center of the lake, trying to wash over me and envelope me in its shapeless form. I didn't dare turn to look at it. I wasn't even sure I would see anything if I did, and somehow that thought was more terrifying. Because I knew I wasn't imagining this. Something was about to happen. But what could I do?

It was far too wet to try to take out my sketchbook now. I was pretty sure even through my jacket and the bag the pages would be damp already. And the inflatable boat beneath me was bucking over the waves too violently for me to draw anything, anyway.

But did my magic actually require pencil and paper? Or could I just focus enough to see my own drawing, even if it were just my finger tracing something through the air?

I wouldn't know until I tried. And I was running out of time to try. The pain in my ears was constant now.

I doubted this would work if the image wasn't very simple, but what immediately leapt to mind was the simplest thing of all to draw: the flat surface of a calm lake.

I didn't open my eyes, just raised my arm and started sketching long, smooth strokes through the air. I could see placid trees on the shore, fluffy clouds in the sky, but mainly the long, flat swells of the lake on a windless, moonless night.

I felt the boat beneath me settling down, and vaguely heard the others yelling as they redoubled their efforts on the oars, pulling us toward shore. But I didn't dare open my eyes. I had to focus on that image, at least until we were safely on dry land.

I heard splashing as some of the others jumped out of the boats, then one last gentle wave lifted the boat beneath me and carried it farther up the gravelly shore.

I opened my eyes, and at once the storm resumed its fearsome pummeling. But the pressure on my ears was gone, and we were on dry ground.

Well, dryish. Snow was already clinging to the rocks, and ice was starting to crust over the little puddles of lake water. I raised my head to look inland but saw only trees whipping fiercely in the wind.

"Ingrid! Come on!" Andrew yelled to me through the roaring wind. I realized I was the only one still sitting in the boat and took his extended hand so he could pull me to my feet. I still moved so awkwardly in the oilskins and overly large boots, but we soon caught up with the others.

We walked together in a tight huddle, through those trees and up a path of wood chips to a large patio. The furniture was covered in weatherproof tarps and stacked against the wall of the house.

I kept my head down as we waited there for a moment, letting the top of my hood take the brunt of the weather. The wind was quieter here. We could probably talk without shouting. And yet none of us said a word, like we were all waiting until we finally got indoors. Maybe the intense shivering took too much out of us. We pressed together like penguins, but I couldn't have distinguished any of us from the rest save possibly Thorbjorn.

Then we were moving again, this time through a doorway and out of the wind. When the last of us was inside and we had shut the door we finally pushed back our hats and looked at each other's red cheeks and plastered hair.

"There's a gas fire in the great room. I'll go fire it up," Adam said. He had been the one to close the door, but now he pushed through all of us to lead the way out of the mudroom. I could see a short hallway that opened up into a larger space, but it was too dark for details.

I stepped out of my boots and shook out of my oilskins, then followed him into the great room. The ceiling vaulted high overhead, and the lake-facing wall was nothing but glass. Not that we could see the lake now; it was lost to the snow-laden winds.

But the wall opposite that glass was one immense fireplace, and it roared to full life at Adam's touch of a button. I could feel the warmth from it already, even across all that open space.

"There's nothing in the kitchen but canned soup and freeze-dried coffee, but-" Adam started to say as he headed towards the kitchen on the north side of the great room.

"You are not going to play the part of our gracious host," Thorbjorn growled at him. Adam froze in mid-gesture towards the cabinets and stove.

"What do you mean? This is my house," he said.

"Your family's house," I said.

"I'm the one who invited you all in," he said. "You promised you'd let this go."

"No, I didn't," I said. "I promised you lawyers once we were back on American soil. But first we all have to decide if we're going to take you back to American soil."

Adam gaped at me for a moment. Then his eye darted over to a cabinet near the doorway to the foyer. He tried to lunge towards it, but Andrew stepped in front of it, pressing his back against the closed doors, and Thorbjorn dropped a hand on Adam's shoulder, first holding him in place and then steering him back to the center of the room, far from any piece of furniture.

"What's happening?" he demanded.

"Justice," Nilda told him. "You are about to face justice."

"We demand it," Kara said to me. "You know we won't find it in that other world. It has to be here, when it's just us."

"I was hoping this would be a council matter," I said.

"How were you hoping to get him there?" Kara asked me.

She had a point. I had no plan for that. Even when the storm blew itself out, our only ride home was the yacht, and we'd need Adam's cooperation for that. I looked to Thorbjorn.

"We will enforce whatever your ruling is," he said. He shot a look at Loke, who was standing near Andrew at the cabinet.

"As much as we can, I suppose," he agreed. But then he turned more serious, all humor gone from his eyes. "It has to be here. I agree with him on that. Judge him, O volva."

"Ingrid?" Andrew said. I looked over to where he was standing, still with his back to the cabinet. "What's going on?"

I didn't know where to even start explaining.

But Jessica did. "Justice," she said, with fierce confidence. "We're here to mete out some justice."

Adam turned even paler. In fact, he looked like he was about to pass out at any moment.

"Get him a chair," I said to Roarr, who nodded and then looked around the room before crossing over to the breakfast bar by the kitchen to bring back one of the tall stools.

"You guys have seen a lot today," I said to my Runde friends. "I don't know what you've made of any of it. I'm sure it's all pretty overwhelming."

"Apparently magic is real," Andrew said, running a hand through his dark blond hair. "And apparently you are quite good at it."

"Not really," I said. "Most of what you've seen was me piggy-backing on other spells. My grandmother's spells."

"Except what you did back there that got us ashore," Tlalli said. "That was all you." She had a look in her eye that I just knew meant the two of us were going to have a much more detailed conversation on that topic later. And I actually really wanted to know how she perceived whatever had happened while we were all on the inflatable boats. Had she felt that thing out over the lake, the thing that had wanted to pull us into it?

There was a tightness to the lines around her mouth that spoke of remembered fear, and I was sure she had.

"Your grandmother is teaching you magic," Jessica said. "But that's not all she does, is it? I know it's a cliche, but in Runde Nora is a pillar of the community. *The* pillar, actually. I guess she's something similar in the other place. That's why these other Vikings are asking you for justice. Because that's what your grandmother does?"

"Villmarkers," Roarr corrected her. "Not Vikings. That's more of a vocation, and not one we engage in anymore."

"Okay," Jessica said with a nod, but her eyes never left me.

"Yes, you're right," I said. "What we are, or she is and I aspire to be, is called a volva. Some people translate that as 'witch', but that's not all we do. We are often asked to make decisions in cases where the truth may require magic to be seen. And sometimes that's in matters of justice, like this one. It's complicated, and now isn't the time for a discussion of the politics of Villmark. Suffice it to say, here, so far from home, I'm the only authority. And even when we get back to Villmark, whatever I declare to be the law here will be honored there."

"So you can execute this man?" Jessica asked, looking towards Adam with deep loathing.

"Well, technically we're in the modern world, where that would be murder," I said. "He's not one of us. I mean, he's not a Villmarker. That complicates things. I'm really just trying to figure out our next steps. Do we leave this to the police, or take it on ourselves? It's not an easy thing to decide, but because it crosses the boundary between the two worlds, it's something that I have to do."

"Lisa," Michelle said as if an understanding had just dawned on her. "Lisa was of our world. Was her murderer of yours?"

"Yes," I said, so grateful to finally be able to tell them the truth. "Yes, she was. And she has been punished, the murderer Halldis. Lisa's soul found peace. I know that for a fact. I'm so sorry I couldn't tell you all before."

"Did you tell her parents?" Jessica asked.

"No, we couldn't," I said.

"But her mother sensed it, I guess," Jessica said. "Maybe I did too. I felt like when I dreamed of Lisa, that she was in a good place, and she wanted me to be happy. But then I'd wake up and remembered the killer had never been caught, and I'd get angry all over again."

"But not anymore, right?" Michelle said, giving her friend a hug. "You can be at peace too now."

"I will be," Jessica agreed, squeezing Michelle tightly. "Just as soon as I see justice served here. Go ahead, Ingrid. We'll all be over here if you need us, but you have a job to do."

"I do," I agreed. "Thanks, you guys. For being so cool about all of this."

Jessica and Michelle smiled and nodded, then settled themselves on a low couch near the fire. Tlalli reached out to squeeze my hand, and Jesús gave me a slap on the shoulder. Then they too headed over to the couch.

I looked up at Andrew. "Are you okay with all this?"

"I have questions," he admitted. "A lot of questions."

"Once we get home again, I'll make the time to give you answers," I promised.

"I hope so," he said with almost scary intensity. But then he said, "if Loke can watch this cabinet, I'll make myself useful in the kitchen. Hot soup all around, I think."

"Thank you," I said. The idea of something warm in my belly was a comforting one, although I doubted I'd have time for soup until after all this was over.

"I got this," Loke said, leaning against the cabinet doors and lazily crossing his arms. "And you've got the volva thing. After what you did out on the lake, this should be a piece of cake." His eyes were smiling at me, but his face too had a tightness of remembered fear. Tlalli wasn't the only one besides me who had felt that thing out on the water, coming for us.

I only wished I believed I had done more than buy us a little time.

CHAPTER 23

"**Y**ou can't do this," Adam said as I finally turned my attention back to him. He still looked like he might vomit at any moment. Some of that was the alcohol, but some of it was raw fear.

I mean, most people would be frightened with four large, heavily armed warrior-types hovering around them menacingly. Even Nilda and Kara were taller than he was, and they clearly knew how to use those knives.

But Adam being horrifically afraid wasn't the best way to get through the next hour. I had to calm him down.

"I know this doesn't make sense to you," I said. "If Gullveig had been just an ordinary young woman, this would all be different. But she wasn't. She belonged to my people, and my people have a different standard of justice than you're used to. I do promise I'll be fair, even though she was a friend of mine."

"But, my lawyers?" he said desperately.

"You won't need them here," Roarr said. Then he picked up another of the tall stools and carried it to a spot at the center of the room, closer to the fire. He raised an eyebrow at me as if questioning the placement, and I gave him a nod.

"I'll need a moment," I said, pulling the crossbody strap of my art bag up over my head. It tangled with the wet mass of my hair, and once I had set the bag on the floor, I shook out my hair as well as I could. I wanted to look at least halfway presentable, even if I was wearing damp jeans, an untucked flannel shirt, and absolutely miserable-looking wool socks. Not remotely volva-like. But I had made do before.

Finally, I settled myself on the stool, sketchpad on my lap, art bag on the ground at my feet.

"What's going on?" Adam asked, but didn't fight as Thorbjorn once more rested a hand on his shoulder to keep him in his seat.

I could feel the fire warm against my back and see the flickering light from the flames reflecting off all the surfaces around me, but Adam was in my shadow. The Runde crowd were either behind me or in the shadows like Loke. Roarr, Nilda and Kara had moved to sit cross-legged on the floor behind the accused, their weapons arrayed on the floor before them.

"The last time I did this, my audience was trolls," I said conversationally as I sketched out myself as a volva. The stool I was sitting on became the more customary three-legged stool of old. Then I drew a cloak of feathers to replace my loose flannel shirt, and the pencil in my sketched version's hand transformed into a bronze wand.

When I looked up, Adam was cowering on his stool before me, and I knew that the pattern of fire behind me had become something more in his vision. "You see me as I am, Adam?" I asked him. I could hear my voice amplified by the volva effect, as I called it, making it ring clearly throughout the room. He nodded.

Then I glance back at my friends and saw Michelle and Jessica hugging each other as they stared at me with wide eyes. Jesús and Tlalli looked deeply impressed, but less surprised.

Andrew standing at the stove in the kitchen looked awe-struck, and a little afraid.

"I suppose I should say something to explain all this," I said, gesturing with my pencil. I hadn't intended that to be frightening, I was just making a rolling motion with my hand to illustrate "all this", but Adam flinched. I just bit back the word "sorry." If I was going to set aside my feelings about Gullveig, I would have to avoid feeling sympathy for poor Adam as well. "You're not on trial here. This is more like an inquest. Do you know what that means?" I asked.

Adam licked his lips nervously, but sounded perfectly calm when he replied, "why don't you tell me what *you* mean by it?"

"There has been a death. This inquest is to determine the nature of that death and what next steps will follow on that," I said. "We are in Canada now, and will remain here until the storm breaks."

"I hope you don't think I'm sailing you back home on my yacht," he said.

"We have friends with cars," I said. "Your cooperation is not required to get us home. But as I was saying, we're in Canada. Turning you in to the Canadian authorities is an option, but it would complicate things. So we have two options I'm currently considering. We bring you back to the United States and turn you in to the authorities there. That would be when your lawyers come in," I added. I expected a smirk or something at that, but he didn't react. "Or we take you back to Villmark and present you to the council. I can't say what happens next if we turn you over to US authorities, but in the case of Villmark, that's where you'd get your trial."

"But not your lawyers," Roarr said.

"No, no lawyers there," I said. "They wouldn't be able to help you there, anyway."

"Take me to the US authorities," Adam said, throwing up his hands. "Let them look at the evidence. They'll conclude what I've already told you: that she killed herself when she jumped off my boat. There was nothing I could've done about it. It was tragic, certainly, but absolutely not my fault. They couldn't possibly find me guilty. You all, on the other hand, I can get put away for kidnapping at least."

"You piloted us here of your own free will," Loke pointed out.

"That doesn't matter," Roarr said. "None of that matters if we take him to Villmark. Which, if he's going to make threats-"

I held up a hand, and he obediently stopped talking, but I could see his words put Adam on edge.

189

"We've heard your story," I said. "Did you have anything further to say? Any details you want to clarify before I go on?"

He opened his mouth, but as he did so I shifted my weight on the stool. Not on purpose, it just wasn't the most comfortable place to sit ever. But when I moved, the sketchpad on my lap tipped and I caught it with the side of my right hand. The hand that stilled held a pencil.

Whatever Adam was seeing in volva-vision must have looked more aggressive than I would've intended, because he snapped his mouth shut again and only answered me with a quick shake of the head.

"All right. Let's go over the facts. Gullveig was on your boat on the evening in question. You don't dispute that fact. Then, for reasons which are still unclear, she struck you across the face then jumped overboard to swim to shore. You didn't go after her or even watch to make sure she reached safety, you just left."

"She made her own choices," Adam said.

"She did, as best as she was able in that moment," I said. "But we know she had a small amount of alcohol in her system, along with a large amount of a drug of the same type as what I found in your medicine cabinet at home."

"You can't prove I gave it to her," Adam said. "Not in a real court of law, you can't."

"Again, that part comes later," I said. "All I'm determining is where justice will best be served. In what world."

"She must've felt the drug," Kara said quietly. "She was on the boat sipping champagne or whatever. Drugged champagne. She must've felt it hitting her. She knew it was more than the wine. Is that when she struck you?"

Adam scowled but said nothing.

"Would she hit him for that?" Nilda pondered. "Gullveig never liked violence. She always found another way. Especially not when she could see the shore, there within reach, why didn't she just try to flee?"

"Did you try to stop her?" I asked Adam. He wouldn't meet my eyes. "She felt the drug working and knew she'd be helpless soon. She wanted to make a run for it, but you tried to keep her on the boat."

"Maybe I was trying to save her from drowning in the lake? Did you ever think of that?" he spat at me.

Loke scoffed. "Not when you say it like that. I'd say it's more likely than ever you just didn't want her to leave. What was your plan? Just sit on her until the drug took the last of her fight away?"

Adam didn't answer, but we could all see it was because Loke was hitting pretty close to the mark.

"She thought she could make it to shore," Kara said softly. "On a normal day, she easily could. Maybe she thought if she was fast enough, she could get there before the drug incapacitated her. She must've fought so hard against that drug, and against the numbing cold of the lake. I wonder how far she got? But you didn't look. You can't tell us even that much."

"Your actions led to her death," I said. "On that we all agree. The problem is, if we turn you over to the police, even if they build a case against you, I'm sure your family's lawyers will make it all go away. No witness but you, and you come from such a good family. Too much doubt with no one able to speak for Gullveig."

He folded his arms and looked away from me without answering. But his defiance wasn't as cocky as before. Had he slumped a little when I said "good family?" What did that mean? Was he not so sure about the power of his lawyers now?

But before I could follow up on that thought, Roarr was saying, "if you are tried before the council in Villmark, you will be found guilty, and you will die."

"There's no death penalty in Minnesota," Adam said.

"Villmark isn't in Minnesota," Roarr growled, but again stopped when I held up a hand.

"This is my dilemma," I said. "One sentence seems too light, the other too heavy. But I must decide what to do, before this storm breaks."

"Luckily, this storm looks like it's going to linger at least into tomorrow," Loke said.

"Yes," I said. I stretched out with my magical senses, but the thing I had felt before was gone now. Or hiding. The storm that was lashing the shore was entirely mundane, if no less dangerous for all that.

"Before I make a decision, I want to speak with some of you privately," I said, sliding down off the stool. My volva illusion broke with that movement, and I was once more just their friend, ordinary Ingrid Torfa. "I just want to have a sense of what everyone is feeling. Like getting impact statements before sentencing. Jessica and Michelle? I'd like to start with you."

"What about me?" Adam asked.

"I'll talk to you last," I said. "Do you have an office or something in this house?"

He pointed to a door next to the cabinet where Loke stood, and I nodded my thanks.

When I opened the door, I saw a room lined with bookshelves. There was no desk, but a few chairs were arranged around a coffee table, and I had Michelle and Jessica join me on those.

"Do you do this a lot?" Michelle asked after I had shut the door.

"Not really," I admitted. "Just once, actually."

"But with trolls?" she pressed.

"That's a long story, but yes," I said. "I should probably warn you, that was for the man who had killed Garrett Nelsen. The trolls were helping him escape. Thorbjorn and his brothers stopped that, but in the end I sentenced him to exile. Exile in the same place he was trying to escape to. I can understand if that feels to you like I let him get away."

I looked from Michelle to Jessica, waiting for a sign from them. Were they angry I had done that? Were they going to demand an explanation? Or assurances that I wouldn't do it again this time with Adam?

But in the end, it was Jessica who spoke. And all she said was, "Thorbjorn has brothers? Plural? More than that one guy we met behind the waterfall?"

"Four of them," I said.

"Do they all look like that?" Michelle asked.

"A couple of them are a little taller," I said.

They both looked at each other, their mouths not quite hanging open.

But then they snapped back to the matter at hand. "Look, we knew Gullveig a little, and we did find her body, so I guess you could say what happens with Adam impacts us. But she was more Nilda's and Kara's friend. We want justice, of course, but we're not the victims here."

"I know," I said. "I really just wanted to take a minute to explain about Lisa."

And then I told them everything. How I had investigated the murder, how I had nearly died when the killer found me first and lured me into a trap, how my grandmother had been the one to act as volva after I was rescued and the killer was detained.

"Halldis was found guilty," I said. "But not just for the murder. She had been manipulating people and was a danger to the community. But my grandmother didn't think she should be executed. Instead, she is being held in a prison cell, magically warded to protect others from her influence."

Of my doubts that those wards were working to full capacity, I said nothing.

"And Roarr?" Jessica asked. "He was being controlled the whole time by this witch Halldis?"

"I don't know for sure," I said honestly. "I don't think he does either. I know he's probably going to continue mourning Lisa forever."

"I don't know how I feel about that," Jessica said. "It feels like he should've done some time. Accessory to murder or something. Nothing happened to him?"

"Nothing but the torture of his own guilty conscience," Michelle said before I could speak. "Have you looked into his eyes? The man is a wreck."

Jessica humphed but said no more.

I next called Tlalli and Jesús into the library.

"I mostly wanted to talk with Tlalli," I admitted. "But I figured you'd want your brother here for support."

"Thank you," she said.

"I want to know what you're thinking about the choice before me," I said. "He stalked you. He drove your roommate away and tormented you for weeks. Also, I'm looking to you to speak for all the other women who aren't here to speak for themselves. I know you talked with a lot of them. What do you think?"

Tlalli looked down at her hands twisted together in her lap. Jesús reached over to put his own hand on hers and she leaned her head against his shoulder briefly.

But then she looked up at me with the gleam of unshed tears in her eyes. "I think you have a very tough choice. But I trust you to make the right one. And if you aren't sure, I know you have the power to call on whatever means you require to guide you."

"You mean that drawing thing she does?" Jesús asked.

"I mean that drawing thing she does," Tlalli agreed.

"I'll do my best to be worthy of the faith you're putting in me," I said as we all got to our feet. But as they were heading out the door, I caught Tlalli's arm to whisper into her ear, "and we have to talk later about... well, everything."

She nodded.

Nilda and Kara kept their interview so brief we never even sat down in the chairs. Like Tlalli, they were placing their faith in my ability to choose wisely.

A nervous sweat was breaking out all over my body. What if I messed this up?

Roarr was lurking outside the door when I opened it to let Nilda and Kara out.

"I don't need to make a statement," he told me. "You know how I feel already."

"You don't want to sway me in one direction or the other?" I asked.

He shook his head. "No. It's not my place. Especially considering..." But he never finished his thought. His role in the other murder, his outsider status, it didn't really matter. He was stepping back from this one.

Which was a relief. He was the only one I had been afraid would demand blood for blood. But he just crossed the room to lean against the breakfast bar and watch Andrew in the kitchen.

"Thorbjorn?" I called. He looked up, startled.

"I have felt no special impact in this matter," he said.

"I know. I just need to talk with you. Loke and Roarr can watch Adam."

"And me," Andrew said. He came out of the kitchen and took Thorbjorn's place glowering over Adam.

"I'm not sure what you need me to say," Thorbjorn said as we both sat down. "I'm sorry about what happened to Gullveig. Perhaps if I had been closer to home, I would've sensed her distress. But I'll never know, will I?"

"Your brother Thormund was at the bonfire that night," I said. "If you could've felt something if you had been there, wouldn't he have when he was?"

"Yes, you're right," he said, but I don't think I had made him feel any better.

"I actually wanted to talk to you about the council," I said. "You know them better than I do. Are they going to be angry about what I'm doing here?"

"That's not what they'll be angry about," he said. "That part they'll understand."

"Even if I choose to turn him over to US authority and not theirs?"

"Even then," he said. "It is your duty as a volva to make such decisions. They won't second guess you."

"I guess that's good to know," I said. "But all the people who know about Villmark now; that's going to be a problem."

"You probably shouldn't have mentioned it in front of Adam," he chastised me.

"Well, at that point we'd taken five people on a mini-tour of Villmark's outlying points of interest, and he must've seen us arrive on a Viking ship, so it felt like the harm was already done," I said.

"It was your grandmother's call," Thorbjorn said. "She had seen you'd need help from both sides to catch this guy. I believed her, so I agreed. But the council might be more skeptical."

"She saw, like she can see the future?" I asked.

Thorbjorn shrugged. "I don't know how she knows what she knows. I just believe in her."

"I do, too," I said. Although unlike Thorbjorn, I wanted to know how she knew things. To me, it mattered.

"What are you going to do?" he asked.

"The only thing I can do," I said with a sigh.

Then we went back out into the main room, and I got back on my stool. I didn't recast the volva spell, though. My words had weight enough.

"I've made my decision," I told Adam. I sensed the others shifting in their seats, turning their attention to me. I felt all their eyes on me.

"Let's have it," he said. He looked exhausted, slumped over on the stool as if he were about to spill onto the floor. But he straightened himself up to hear my verdict.

"When the storm breaks, we are all going back to the United States, and you will turn yourself in to the authorities. You will tell them everything that you did."

"I didn't kill her," he interjected.

"So say that," I said. "But tell them everything you told me. Or as much as your family's lawyers advise you to, I guess. What I'm saying is, you will go through that system in the proper way and accept that system's outcome."

"What if I get off? What will you do then?" he asked.

"I'll accept it," I said. "That's the whole point of this. I'm turning you over to that justice system, for all its strengths and flaws."

"Fine," he said, throwing up his hands in disgust. "What a waste of an evening."

"We kept you from fleeing to Canada," Andrew said. "Or coming here just to flee farther away. You're going home now. That's all we wanted."

"Whatever," Adam said. "Now, I'm going to bed."

He started to slide off the stool, but Thorbjorn restrained him with one hand on his shoulder. "She isn't finished," he said.

"No, there's one thing more," I said. "You will accept the outcome of the US justice system, whatever it is. You won't try to flee again." Then I summoned every bit of the volva-effect as I leaned in to him, my voice booming although I wasn't raising it. I think my eyes might've gotten a little crazy as well, the way he tried to shrink away from me. But Thorbjorn held him steady. "And, Adam? You won't speak of who we are or where we're from to anyone. Anyone. Do you understand?"

"Who would ever believe me?" Adam scoffed. "You people are nuts."

"Listen," I said. I kept staring straight into his eyes until he stopped trying to dismiss me. Until he took me seriously. "You've not seen much, but you've seen enough to know I speak the truth when I tell you this," I said. "If you whisper a word to anyone I will know. And I and my people will come for you. There will be nowhere for you to hide. And you will regret the moment you ever crossed us. Are we clear?"

"Yes," he said, his voice cracking. Then he licked his lips and tried again. "Yes. I understand."

"I hope you do," I said.

CHAPTER 24

$\mathcal{T}$he storm broke in the early hours of the morning, and Adam only agreed to take us all back home again on the yacht because he didn't want to leave it anchored off shore. He was lucky it had survived the night.

Or so he said. Myself, I was pretty sure it had not been just luck. I could sense the remnants of spells all around it, my magic and Tlalli's. That was what had kept the yacht sound and afloat throughout the night.

As we made our way south back to the marina in Duluth, I spent as much time as I could stand up on the deck, the cold wind in my face as I tried to sense what had tried to swallow us all up the night before.

I couldn't feel it anywhere, but my gut was sure it was still there, hiding.

And that it had waited until we were nearly ashore to make its move, because that move had been only a warning.

But a warning of what?

It might be safer for me to stay off the lake. Which, given that it was nearly winter, would be easy enough to do after this last boat ride. But by spring I would have to be much stronger with my magic.

Much, much stronger.

As we approached the marina, Tlalli came up on deck to stand beside me, leaning on the rail looking out towards the cold heart of the steel gray lake.

"Jesús and I would like to go back up to Runde with you after we're ashore and Adam is in custody," she said. "We have a van. It's cold and prone to breaking down, but it'll fit everybody."

"Oh, yeah," I said. I had forgotten that our cars were back in Runde. And the Viking ship was in pieces strewn over the bottom of the lake. My heart clenched at the thought.

"I wanted to talk with your grandmother," she went on.

"Of course," I said. "We'll be there before dusk, I'm sure. You can watch us do the spells and then ask us anything. I can't promise we have all the answers, but we'll do our best. And by 'we' I of course mean my grandmother."

"It's good you have her," Tlalli said. "Not just as family, but as a teacher. Treasure that."

"I try to," I said.

"It looks like we don't need to worry about getting a ride out of the marina," Loke said as he appeared suddenly at the top of the ladder from below deck. He pointed in the direction we weren't looking, and we joined him at that rail.

We were nearly at the marina, and beyond that we could see the parking lot was filled with police cars.

"Are they here for us?" I asked. "Did someone call ahead?"

"No. Well, Adam wanted to call his father from the yacht and have him come down to pick him up," Loke said. "Maybe that's him there by the black sedan. I doubt he called the cops, though."

"If they suspected him and knew he took the yacht, I'm sure they knew how to find him better even than Andrew did," Tlalli said. "Maybe they knew he was in Canada. And then he just turned around and came home. I wonder what they made of that?"

"If that's true, we never needed to get involved at all, then," I said, feeling suddenly tired. "They tracked him down without us."

"Don't be silly," Tlalli said. "Without us, Adam would still be in Canada. He'd hear that the police were on to him while he was still in his family's cabin. He'd see the news or hear from friends or something. And what then? Do you think without us with him he'd come back and face the music? Or would he've kept running?"

"Personally, I think they'd catch him no matter where he went," Loke said. "He's not built for a life on the run."

"I think he might've turned himself in," I said. They both looked at me as if pitying my naivety, but that was truly what I felt. "I don't agree that Gullveig's death was an accident, but I really think that Adam believes that's true. And he wants his day in court so they can validate his belief. But I guess we'll never know for sure what he would've done without us. We chose to act."

The police arrested Adam the moment he stepped off the yacht, but the man by the sedan had indeed been his father. He had three lawyers with him already, and they were clearly already annoying the police officers. But Adam didn't seem pleased to see them, and the look on his father's face when he saw his son being cuffed by the police was not one of righteous indignation. It was resigned disappointment.

Maybe that was why Adam hadn't seemed entirely sure he was getting off scot free. Whatever the courts decided, if it ever even made it that far, he had already diminished himself in his father's eyes. And that mattered to him.

I wasn't sure how the police would react to our presence, but total indifference hadn't been any of the scenarios that had been playing through my mind. As it turned out, they had already spoken to the guard who had been on duty the day before. And so the lot of us were only so many partygoers in their eyes, just another of the many anonymous throngs that Adam brought out to his family's yacht several times a week. After they had Adam in custody, they blocked the yacht off as a potential crime scene but just told the rest of us to get on our way.

We had to hail a ride to Tlalli and Jesús' apartment, then pile into their van for the cold ride back to Runde. None of us had slept well in Canada, and it was a quiet stretch of hours.

Once back in town we went our separate ways to shower and

change our clothes. Tlalli and Jesús had grabbed clothes from home when we'd picked up their van, and I let them use the shower at my grandmother's cabin. Then we three walked together towards the meeting hall to meet back up with the others.

"I see two overlapping places," Tlalli said to me as we walked down the road towards the hall. "That's different than the pocket magic my ancestors did."

"Look up towards the top of the waterfall," I said. "I have a hard time sensing it, but sometimes I can see like a shimmer."

"I see... something," she said. "Oh. Yes. That's the pocket there. Can I get a closer look?"

"That I don't know," I said. "This might not be a good time."

"There are consequences to you showing us everything and taking us out on that ship," she guessed.

"Yes. And soon I'll know what they are," I said. "But I'm sure there will be a better day soon for you to come back up and get the full tour."

"I can wait," she said. "Now that I know this is here, it's like so much anxiety is just lifted off my shoulders. I thought I had locked myself out of my true home and I'd never find the key again. I don't have my answers yet, but now I finally feel like I will. Someday. I didn't feel that way two days ago."

My grandmother was already inside waiting for us. Tlalli and Jesús sat at one of the tables at the edge of the room and watched as the two of us cast the spells to turn the drab meeting hall into the Viking long-house that was our mead hall.

At almost the same second as we had finished our work, the front door burst open, and Andrew, Michelle, Jessica and Loke came inside.

"Go ahead and say hello to your friends," my grandmother told me. "I'm going to take Tlalli downstairs for a bit. We have a lot to discuss."

"Okay," I said, at first stunned and then a little jealous that Tlalli was about to go down to the cellar.

I'd never been invited down to the cellar.

Then the back door opened and Roarr came inside, followed by Nilda and Kara. The door swung nearly closed and my heart sank a little, but then it was flung open again and Thorbjorn came inside. I hadn't even realized I had been waiting for him to appear, or had been so sure he wouldn't.

"Hey, Ingrid," Andrew said as he approached me, and I turned to give him a smile of greeting. He had two mugs of steaming cider in his hands but for the longest time just stood there looking at me like he was turning something over in his mind.

"Is one of those for me?" I asked at last.

"Oh. Yeah," he said, looking down at the mugs in his hands.

"Let's sit by the fire," I said. "I'm still cold in my bones from being out on the lake despite the world's longest, hottest shower."

"Well, you were up on the deck the whole ride home," he chided me.

"Not the *whole* ride," I said.

We sat down at the end of one of the long tables, across from each other, although we weren't looking at each other. I took a sip of the spiced cider as I looked around the room. Jesús and Loke were talking together, grinning and laughing in a way that made me wonder if I should be worried that they were suddenly thick as thieves. But as I couldn't quite figure out which one was the bad influence and which the potentially influenced, I decided to leave it alone.

Roarr was sitting alone with a mug of beer, but that was normal for him. After everything that followed his talking with Gullveig at the party days before, I couldn't blame him for regressing back to solitude.

Nilda and Kara were sitting with Michelle and Jessica, and from the snatches of their conversation that I could overhear, the two Vill-markers were telling the Runde women about all the things they were going to show them when they came up to the village.

But was that actually going to happen? I knew Lisa had been up in the village, and I knew there were other Runde people who had been up there in the past. But I didn't think that had ever been more than a few individuals moving on their own. I don't think it had ever been a group activity. Would all my friends suddenly get a free pass between the two worlds?

Then I saw Thorbjorn walking towards me and Andrew with his customarily large mug of beer in his hands. He had come down the center of the room, which put him on Andrew's side of the table. He hesitated for a moment, then stepped over the bench to sit beside Andrew and take a sip of his beer. Then he looked up at me, then over at Andrew, as if trying to guess what sort of conversation we'd been having before he joined us.

Only we hadn't been talking at all. It was all so awkward.

Damn Loke and his insidious comments. Andrew and Thorbjorn weren't mirror versions of each other. Maybe it would be simpler if they were.

"So, what happens now?" Andrew asked. He looked at me, then at Thorbjorn.

Then I realized what was going on. And I knew this was coming to me so belatedly that I felt my cheeks flush when I finally figured it out.

Both Andrew and Thorbjorn were trying to gauge without saying anything out loud what relationship the other one had with me.

And I didn't even know the answer to that one.

"Ingrid?" Thorbjorn asked.

"I don't know," I said, putting my hands over my cheeks and hoping any flush they might've seen could be written off as a reaction to the alcohol in the cider.

The very small amount of alcohol in the cider.

"I guess it's good that things are all out in the open now, right?" Andrew said. "I mean, now I know why you're never around. I guess you're in that other place." He glanced over at Thorbjorn, then turned his attention back to his cider.

I wanted to say that I wasn't with Thorbjorn every time I went to Villmark, but I couldn't find a way to phrase it that wouldn't possibly hurt Thorbjorn's feelings. I had to say something else.

"Have you heard anything from the council?" I asked Thorbjorn, although I was dreading his answer.

"They are aware," he said, frowning into his beer. "That's all I've heard."

"Is that a good thing? That silence?" I asked.

"It means they are considering things," he said. "We won't know what they decide until they tell us. But it's not unheard of for people from the outside to know of our existence. And trusted people move between the worlds all the time. Lisa did. I'm sure if you wanted to bring your friends to see your home in town, that would be acceptable." He glanced over at Andrew, who was still looking fixedly down at his cider. Then he looked back at me with a warning in his eyes, "not the cabin in the woods."

"No, we agreed about that," I promised him. Now it was Andrew's turn for the furtive looks again.

This was going to drive me crazy.

"Ingrid!" I looked up to see Tlalli and Jesús both standing over me and, grateful for the interruption, I got up from the bench. Tlalli pulled me into a tight hug.

"She's overwhelmed," Jesús told me when Tlalli just kept squeezing me without speaking.

"I guess," I said.

But then Tlalli finally let me go, wiping at her eyes as she stepped back. "Your grandmother is an amazing woman."

"She is," I agreed.

"She's given me some books and other things to help me rediscover my own magic," she said. "She's even given me the name of a witch who lives in Duluth who can help me."

"Wow," I said. "I didn't know my grandmother even knew anyone in Duluth. Or that there were other witches."

"She's Irish," Tlalli told me. "Saoirse Duncan."

"Irish?"

"Well, Celtic, I guess. The magic she practices is older than calling that island Ireland," Tlalli said. Then she laughed. "Two days ago, I thought the only place with real magic was México. Then I learn about this place, and now there's even more. So many more."

"That's news to me too," I said. "It *is* overwhelming."

"I know! But I'll be calling you, okay?" she said. "We have to head back to Duluth now. Work and school in the morning. But your grandmother says we'll be able to reach your phone now."

"Yes, we definitely have to stay in touch. You, too," I added to Jesús. "Not everything in life is magic, after all."

"No, that's true," he said. We'd reached the doorway, and he pulled me into a quick hug then whispered into my ear, "but if all of this helps my sister and I find our mother again? Nothing is more important than that."

"I hope you do," I said, and now I was the one wiping tears from my eyes.

Then they were gone, and I turned back to the table where I had left Andrew and Thorbjorn sitting together. Awkward was too small a word.

"Decisions, decisions," Loke said. As usual, he had just appeared at my elbow as if he had always been there.

"What are on about?" I asked.

He just tipped his head towards Andrew and Thorbjorn.

"You don't think I have more important things to worry about?" I asked. "If the events from yesterday mean anything, they mean that I need to double-down on my studies. I need more knowledge and more skill. That's going to have to take all my time."

"No more art?" he asked, which surprised me. I thought he was going to stick to ribbing me about my love life. But this wasn't ribbing. He sounded really concerned.

"My art is part of my magic," I said. "But if you mean will I continue pursuing it as a career out in this world?"

But I couldn't answer my own question. And I wiped another tear from my eye.

But I was scarcely the only twenty-something who had to give up on their dreams when the responsibilities started mounting.

"You'll always have your art," Loke said, his dark brown eyes completely sincere. "The form might change, but it's a part of you."

"I know," I said.

"But as to those two," he said, and that gleam of mischief was back.

"Oh, stop," I said.

"You've never asked me," he said with a sly grin.

I gave in. "Never asked you what?"

"Why I call Andrew your Runde Thorbjorn, but I never call Thorbjorn your Villmark Andrew." He was grinning at me as if he had just scored a huge point.

"What does that even mean?" I asked, but then threw up my hands. "Never mind. You know what? I no longer want to know what you're thinking."

I just saw his mouth drop open, appalled at my response, but only in a brief glimpse before I turned my back on him and went back to my seat at the table across from Andrew and Thorbjorn.

I did not have to choose between my friends.

CHAPTER 25

Three days later, I finally got my first look at the inside of the council hall.

It was impressive. In size it rivaled my grandmother's mead hall, the bottom of the thatched roof above lost in the shadows beyond the carved rafters. Although the thatching was newish, the woodwork was old. The techniques used to work the twisting serpents and sleek wolves and ever-present knot-work were far simpler than what Solvi had used. Cruder, formed with less delicate tools. I could see a few faint hints of pigment in some of the carvings, as if they had once been painted but centuries ago.

I had a lot of time to admire the building while the council kept me waiting. I knelt on the floor and tried not to fidget. I was dressed in Villmarker clothes, and although Nilda and Kara nearly always wore pants, I had opted for the more old school traditional dress and apron. I guessed I looked okay. I really wished my grandmother was there with me, but she had left me at the door, sending me in alone.

And her last words were, "there's really nothing I can do to prepare you for this."

That was really what she said. How did that help? Unless her plan was to make me a nervous wreck. In that case, she had scored high marks.

There was a rustle of noise and I looked up to see the curtain at the back of the raised dais moving. Then Thorbjorn's father emerged, crossing the dais to take his place at the farthest of the three low stools lined up in front of the Villmark pillars.

These weren't the ones Torfa had brought with her from the old world. Those were in my grandmother's house in town. If these belonged to any particular family, which they must have done, I had no idea which family it was. But they were impressive, the wood a dark, rich shade of brown.

I should know whose they were, and where they had come from originally. It was probably politically important. Ugh, there was so much I still didn't know.

The curtain parted again and the only woman on the council stepped through. Her silver hair was neatly arranged in a thin braid that wrapped several times around her head in an elaborate crown, and she was wearing rings on every finger with multiple rings on some fingers. She sat down on the middle stool.

She was immediately followed by the oldest member of the council, a stooped old man with sparse but wild hair that formed a white halo around his grizzled scalp. He leaned heavily on a staff as he lowered himself to his own stool. The other two looked on with gentle concern, and he gave them both a curt nod once he was settled.

"Ingrid Torfudottir," Thorbjorn's father said, his voice filling the hall as if he were booming the words out, although he was speaking relatively quietly since it was just the four of us.

"That is I," I said in my most carefully pronounced Villmarker Norse.

"We have agreed to proceed in English," the woman told me. She spoke as if she were granting me a great boon. Which she really was.

"Thank you," I said, first in Norse and then in English.

"We're much delayed in meeting with you," the old man said. "That was deliberate, and we will not apologize."

"We know much about you all the same," Thorbjorn's father said.

"You are acquainted with my sons. I'm sure they have told you some about me."

"Not really," I admitted. "I don't even know your name."

He blinked at me in surprise. "Well, we'll have to remedy that first. I am Valki."

"Brigida," the woman said, touching one be-ringed finger to her heart.

"Haraldr," the old man said.

"It's an honor to meet you," I said. Was I supposed to bow or something?

"We have made certain decisions regarding you," Valki said. He made no effort to make those words sound less ominous.

"But first we would like to hear from you," Brigida said. "What are your intentions?"

"What do you mean?" I asked. "What intentions? Do you mean here, now, in this room, or...?"

But none of them answered, or let their facial expressions give me even the tiniest of hints.

I swallowed hard and rubbed my sweaty palms on my apron. I couldn't tell them what they wanted to hear if I had no idea what that was. And it would be a really bad idea to go all in on a guess.

So I would just have to decide what that question meant to me and answer honestly.

"I intend to someday take my grandmother's place as volva," I said. None of their faces so much as twitched the corner of their mouth or blinked an eye. "But that's far in the future, I know that. In the meantime, I intend to help my grandmother as much as I can, as much as she needs. I know she's been getting on fine without me all this time, and I guess she got on fine without my mother since the day she left here. So when I say 'as much as she needs,' I'm not lying to myself that the amount she needs me is not much. Not yet. But she might need me more in the future. I expect she will. And I intend to be ready when she does."

They still didn't move in the slightest. Apparently I was supposed to say more?

"Um, so I guess right now my intention is to study as much as I can. Really buckle down and focus. And, um, work on my Norse. More."

There was another long moment where they didn't respond, but this time I wasn't going to fill the silence. I could wait as long as they could.

"Very well," Brigida said at last, with a quick glance to the men on either side of her. "Now we will speak."

I nodded and tried not to look too eager, or too scared out of my mind.

"You have been an absolute force of chaos since the moment you arrived in the town down the hill, in Runde," she said. "You wander in and out of the worlds at will. You keep company with at least one highly questionable individual. You go all in following your grandmother's worst instincts." The old man Haraldr murmured something, and she listened, nodding, then added, "and your magic is sloppy and unfocused."

"I thought none of you could do magic," I said.

Which was a huge mistake. The three of them glared down at me with such rancor I immediately dropped my head and stared at the pattern in the wood floorboards in front of my knees.

"Ingrid Torfudottir," Valki said warningly.

"I'm sorry I spoke out of turn," I said, but I kept my head down.

"There are two sides to every coin," he said. "You've also been a help to us in some murder investigations. As well as in issues of trade, which as the others well know are of far greater importance to our people than certain other issues."

I sensed he was airing a little council dirty laundry. Brigida sucked her teeth but didn't argue. And Haraldr just sat quietly. I glanced up to see he had apparently drifted off to sleep. Brigida picked up his staff and nudged him with it, and he woke with a snort.

"Oh, my turn, is it?" he asked. "Chastisement all done?"

"Just get on with your bit," Brigida said.

"Ingrid Torfudottir," he said, slapping his hands down on his knees and leaning forward to make sure I was paying attention. I gave him a little nod. "It has become clear to us, but particularly to me, that your education has been a little slipshod. You could stand to have more guidance, but your grandmother is not the one to provide it. We all know this."

I could scarcely argue with that. I had been feeling the same for a long time. But I wouldn't say those words out loud. I wouldn't betray my grandmother that way, not to these people.

"She has more power than has been seen in generations, but she is losing touch with this world," he went on.

"What?" I gasped. "What are you saying?"

"You are new here and so have nothing to compare to," Valki said. "But we've been observing her for some time. There has been a change."

"We're worried," Brigida said.

"I don't see any sign that she is losing touch," I said. "That doesn't feel true to me. Not at all."

"Doesn't it?" Brigida asked. "Then why do you ask the Thors about the wards that protect us all from Halldis' magic? What is that if not a fear that your grandmother's power is not what it once was?"

"Valkissons," Valki grumbled.

"If you didn't want them to be called the Thors, you shouldn't have named every one of them after the thunder god," Brigida hissed back at him.

"We're worried about your grandmother," Haraldr said with an annoyed glance at the other two. "That's our point."

"But I can't take her place," I said. "I'm not ready. Not remotely."

"Believe me, we know that," Haraldr said. "Hence our decision."

Finally, we were getting to the real point of this meeting. I held my breath, waiting to hear what he was about to say.

"We are prepared to teach you all we know," Haraldr said. "You are correct, I am no wielder of magic in the way your grandmother is, but I am educated in the ways of the volva. That was once my mother's office, and her mother's before her. And I myself am a soothsayer. There is much you can learn from me."

"I'm ready to learn whatever anyone has to teach me," I said truthfully.

"But there are things you must agree to," he said, as if I hadn't spoken at all. "I will teach you the deeper magics even your grand-mother doesn't delve into. I will teach you the secrets of the runes and of bindings and wards. I will teach you to work weal and work woe. I will teach you all of it."

"What must I agree to?" I asked, since he clearly wanted me to.

"First, that when you have learned all that you can from me, you will have to go down into the deepest cave and learn all you can from Halldis. That is the real reason, after all, that she is not dead."

My blood ran cold. And not just at the idea of spending time with that woman, and a lot of time at that. She had offered to teach me before, but I was sure when I had gotten her imprisoned for murder that offer had been taken off the table. She wouldn't want to teach me now. So I was supposed to trick her into it somehow? Or coerce her to?

"Second," Haraldr said, apparently unaware that my mind was still spinning from the first stipulation. "This learning cannot take place in the world where you currently live. You must leave it behind and dwell among us."

"You mean move into Villmark?" I asked. Well, my grandmother already had a house in town, so that was easy, but... "forever?"

"Not forever," Brigida said with something almost like gentleness. "But for some time. For as far into the future as we three can see. You must become more thoroughly one of us than you are now. We will judge when that has happened, and we will not guess now how long that will take."

But from the look on her face, I was pretty sure the time frame she was thinking of wasn't too short from forever.

"Third," Haraldr said. "Well, it really ties in to the second, but we just wish to be clear. You've exposed our existence to a large number of companions in the last few days. We asked your grandmother to wipe the memories from their minds, but she refuses to do so."

After an initial wave of horror, I had to bite down on my lip to keep from smiling at that. I wished I had been there to see my grand-mother when she turned them down. I had no idea they had even been talking with my grandmother, but I was so happy she was looking out for my friends. I needed them.

"It is problematic they even know of our existence, but that is in the past," Haraldr went on. "In the present and into the future, they will be expected to carry on as if they weren't aware."

"What's that mean?" I asked. "They were never going to tell anyone, I promise you."

"It means they won't be passing between the worlds," Brigida said. "No visits. And in particular, no visits to you. As per what I said earlier. We need you to become more thoroughly one of us. You can see how they could interfere with that process."

I nodded that I understood, but I didn't trust myself to try speaking.

"So, think carefully before you answer. Do you agree?" Valki asked.

"What happens if I don't?" I asked. "I mean, can I go on as before, learning from my grandmother?"

"You can do as you like out in that world," Brigida said with a dismissive wave in the general direction of Runde. "But you'll never be welcome back in this one."

"Do you agree?" Valki pressed.

They were all watching me, the weight of their collective gazes pressing down on me. I couldn't breathe. I felt crushed. Physically and emotionally crushed.

"I need to think carefully," I said. "Before I agree, I need to be sure. Can I take a few days?"

This response seemed to please all three of them, and they sat back on their stools as if finally able to relax. So the meeting had been just as tense for them as for me.

"Three days," Valki said. "Return here in three days with your answer."

I nodded, murmured a thank you, then got up and walked back out of the hall, out into the last weak rays of the setting November sun.

CHAPTER 26

$\mathcal{I}$ suppose the plan in my head, if I had even had one, had been to walk with my head down, sadly dragging my feet, all the way through Villmark and down the hill to Runde. Like a defeated and depressed character in a cartoon.

But the minute I stepped out of the council hall and the doors slammed shut behind me with a shattering air of finality, I saw I wasn't alone. Loke was leaning against the fence across the street, apparently waiting for me to come out. And in his arms was Mjolner.

"Hey, you two!" I cried as Mjolner jumped from Loke's grasp to wind back and forth around my ankles. "This is nice, to see you both. It's a welcome reminder that no matter which place I'm in, I can always rely on the company of my two fellow world-hoppers."

"That bad, huh?" Loke said.

"Yeah," I said as I bent to scoop Mjolner up into my arms. "That bad."

Mjolner clearly sensed my mood. Normally he couldn't stand more than a minute of cuddling and hated to be carried around. But instead of pushing away from me, he snuggled his head against the side of my neck and purred loudly.

"Spill," Loke said as we started up the road towards the well that marked the center of town.

"Well, they don't trust my grandmother, that's clear," I said.

"That's always been true," he said diplomatically. "And I'm sorry to tell you, it's not just the council."

"What do you mean?" I asked.

"Well, imagine a continuum," he said, holding his hands up, far apart. "Over here, there's me. Borders are meant to be crossed at will, and might as well not even exist. And over here is Raggi and his ilk. Never cross the borders, they are there for a reason. Blah, blah, blah," he said.

"And?"

"Well, obviously most of this village is in between these two points," he said, gesturing with his hands again. "And there are people all along this continuum. But most people are a lot closer to Raggi than they are to me. Your grandmother, she wanted to change that. Not bring people all the way over to my way of thinking, of course, but maybe a little closer to the middle. She's been trying to change things for decades. But I don't think she's ever had much success at it."

"Everyone thinks I'm going to take over from her, specifically in trying to change things, don't they?" I said with a sigh.

"That's the common assumption on both sides," he said as he thrust his hands into his pockets.

"I don't think I can," I said. "I'm not even sure I want to. I don't know enough yet to say."

"Fair enough," he said with a careless shrug. "Is that what they wanted to talk to you about in there?"

"Partly," I said. Then I told him what the council had offered me, and about the terms, and about what would happen if I turned them down.

When I was done talking he just let out a low whistle but said no more. We walked on in silence, continuing up the road towards the center of town. Only a few people were still out on the streets, and they were all bustling to get home before dusk fully descended on us.

The little bit of snow from the storm had melted, but the temperatures were getting lower and lower at night.

"I have to say yes, don't I?" I said miserably. "I can't say no. I have no real choice here."

"You can walk away from all of this in a hundred different ways," Loke said. "If you like, you can turn around right now and head out into the hills, on into the mountains. Follow the Solvi road." I shot him a look, and he held up his hands in surrender. "Okay, that's one 'no.' But I have ninety-nine more options for you."

"I can't walk away," I said. Then I caught his sleeve to pull him to a stop. Mjolner finally objected to being in my arms and I bent to set him down before saying, "do you think my grandmother is slipping?"

"Mentally?" Loke asked with a frown.

"Yikes," I said. "I meant magically, but maybe I do mean mentally. Aren't they the same?"

"Related," he said. "She might be on a decline, I guess, but if it is, it's a very slow one."

"And as slow as it is, I'm still not stepping up fast enough to help her," I said.

Loke said nothing, just gave me a look that seemed to say, "the answers are within you."

Then I looked up and realized I had stopped our walk right in front of my grandmother's house near the center of Villmark. "I guess I'll be living here now," I said, looking up at the featureless facade in front of me. The windows all had shades carefully drawn down like so many closed eyes.

"You have that cabin in the woods," Loke said.

"I can't go there yet," I said.

"But soon you'll be able to," he said brightly.

"No, I think this is the place, even when I have the power to travel through the woods safely on my own," I sighed. "I'm supposed to be living here to become one of you. I can't do that out in the woods by myself. More's the pity."

"Ingy, I know you're feeling down, but this really isn't so bad," he said. Then he took a step closer to the garden gate. "Come on. Let's go inside."

"Why?" I asked. It felt like intruding, even though it was as much my home as my grandmother's.

"Why not?" he said, grabbing my hand and pulling me after him, through the garden space and up the steps to the front door.

The main floor of the house was one great room with large south-facing windows, but when we stepped inside everything was gloomy and dark. The sun had gone down behind the hills, and the house was cold as well as dark.

It felt empty. Not just that there was sparse furniture and nothing at all decorating the walls. I could just feel in my bones that no one lived here, and no one had lived here in a very long time.

I shivered.

"Hey," Loke said, throwing his arms up dramatically. "It's not much now, but once Nilda and Kara have their way with it, it'll be great. Seriously, let them take over your housewarming party. You'll not regret it."

I gave him a smile. I knew he was right about that. But the smile left me as quickly as it came.

Nilda and Kara would soon be the only friends I'd have around. And they were great, but I was going to miss the others. My Runde crowd.

And I had promised Tlalli and Jesús to stay in touch. I was going to break that promise almost at once. I felt like garbage.

"Hey," Loke said again, a bit less boisterously this time. It was like he could tell his efforts to cheer me just weren't going to cut it. Not today. "Come here." He put an arm around my shoulders and guided me over to the windows. "Drat, it's gotten dark. But still, look down there."

I followed the direction of his finger, down into the valley at the south end of the village, past the public gardens.

"I don't see anything," I said. With the sun behind the hills to the west, the valley was just a pit of darkness that stretched to a bare glimpse of the lake far on the horizon.

"Look carefully," he said. "Follow the road past the garden. It's strewn with white pebbles that reflect the starlight. Do you see it?"

"I think so," I said, squinting.

"Follow that road with your eyes. It breaks in a few places - that's where the hills start to roll - but you can pick up the next stretch if you look carefully."

"Okay," I said. "Cow pastures?"

"And goats and a few pigs," he said. "All the animals safely indoors by now, I'm sure. But do you see that house there? It's apart from the others, not close to the road at all. It's just there, in that stand of trees."

At first I didn't think I could find it. Then I saw a single window glowing with light from a lamp, and once I had that I could discern the outline of the building around it. "Yes, I see it."

"That's my family's house," he said. "That's where I live with my sister, Esja. I know I promised to introduce you two. But she has good and bad days, and lately they've all been bad."

"I'm sorry," I said. "I hope I didn't pressure you. Not when you had so much to deal with it."

"Not at all," he said. "But I'm still waiting for that first good day."

"I'll be there when she's ready," I promised. Then I realized that was as much as promising I was going to be in Villmark and capable of reaching that house when that day came.

So I had already made up my mind. I was going to agree to the council's demands. I had to.

"I hate that house," Loke said. "And yet I can't leave it. Because that house and Esja are like one. If not for Esja I would go far, far away from here, from all this. Further than Duluth or Canada, further than Adam was planning to go in a million years. I don't think I'd ever stop that going away. I know I'd never return."

I didn't know what to say, so I just hugged him as tightly as I could, for as long as he would allow.

Which wasn't long. He really did remind me of Mjolner in a lot of ways.

"But I can't do that, and so here I am!" he said, stepping away from me and swinging his arms as if defining his personal space. "But at least now I have a crucial new job to keep my occupied."

"You've got a job?" I asked. "Doing what?"

"Keeping you connected with your friends, of course," he said. "The council forbids you from seeing them and them from seeing you, but they never said a thing about me doing both."

"I think it was implied," I said.

He waved his hand dismissively. "As much as I hate following rules, I really hate following the rules that are *implied*."

Normally I disapproved of Loke's anarchist worldview, but I had to admit he had me with that one.

"Come on," he said, leading the way back to the front door. "Time to head back to Runde."

"I guess I do have to pack," I said as I trailed along behind him.

He stopped just outside the door to spin on one heel and give me a mock severe look. "Pack? That's what you're thinking of?"

"What are you thinking of?" I asked.

"I'm thinking you have three days to spend in Runde with your Runde friends. That's one long party to be whipped up on short notice, but I think I can manage it."

"I'm exhausted already just thinking about it," I said.

"You can sleep when you're dead," he said with another dismissive wave. "In the mean time, I'm going to be sure you fill every waking minute of the next three days with maximum friends and fun. Hey!" he said, clapping his hands together and tipping his head to give me a conspiratorial wink. "You can call that packing too."

"I guess I can," I said, and found myself smiling, really smiling.

I had a path in front of me, and I couldn't tell how long that path was. But at the end of it, I would be back among my friends again. It shone like an enchanted city on the horizon, my final, most magical destination.

Of course, between me and that final step into the enchanted city was an encounter with Halldis, but I didn't have to think about that now. So I deliberately didn't.

"It's not forever," he said, perhaps misreading the look on my face.

"I know," I said, pushing my fear of Halldis aside. "If I work hard, it will be a lot less than forever, right?"

"Right," he agreed. "And in the meantime, did I mention I am the most discrete carrier of love letters? I rarely steam them open and almost never make copies for my own use."

"What? Ew!" I said, slugging him hard on the arm.

"Oh, you're going to appreciate me before all this is through," he said. "I can guarantee it."

And I knew I would. Not that I would tell him, but I already did.

CHECK OUT BOOK FOUR!

The Viking Witch will return in Killing in the Village Commons, coming February 9, 2021 and available for preorder now!

Winter has come to the lost Norse village of Villmark, the wind and snow separating cozy house from cozy house like a knife breaks apart shortbread.

And for the first time in her life, Ingrid Torfa lives alone. No mother, no grandmother, no roommate. Just a big, empty house and a cat who loves to disappear. Magical studies fill her every waking hour, and yet those hours stretch out in unbroken silence.

Until a scream rents the night, drawing every neighbor out into the cold streets. A woman lies dead at the bottom of the well. It looks like an accident to the villagers, but to Ingrid it feels like a murder.

Luckily, Ingrid knows just the friends to help her solve the mystery. Not even the bite of winter can stop them from uncovering the truth.

Killing in the Village Commons, Book 4 in the Viking Witch Mystery Series!

THE WITCHES THREE COZY MYSTERIES

In case you missed it, check out Charm School, the first book in the complete Witches Three Cozy Mystery Series!

Amanda Clarke thinks of herself as perfectly ordinary in every way. Just a small-town girl who serves breakfast all day in a little diner nestled next to the highway, nothing but dairy farms for miles around. She fits in there.

But then an old woman she never met dies, and Amanda was named in her will. Now Amanda packs a bag and heads to the big city, to Miss Zenobia Weekes' Charm School for Exceptional Young Ladies. And it's not in just any neighborhood. No, she finds herself on Summit Avenue in St. Paul, a street lined with gorgeous old houses, the former homes of lumber barons, railroad millionaires, even the writer F. Scott Fitzgerald. Why, Amanda can practically hear the jazz music still playing across the decades.

Scratch that. The music really, literally, still plays in the backyard of the charm school. Because the house stretches across time itself. Without a witch to protect this tear in the fabric of the world, anything can spill over. Like music.

Or like murder.

Charm School, the first book in the complete Witches Three Cozy Mystery Series!

ALSO FROM RATATOSKR PRESS

The Ritchie and Fitz Sci-Fi Murder Mysteries starts with Murder on the Intergalactic Railway.

For Murdina Ritchie, acceptance at the Oymyakon Foreign Service Academy means one last chance at her dream of becoming a diplomat for the Union of Free Worlds. For Shackleton Fitz IV, it represents his last chance not to fail out of military service entirely.

Strange that fate should throw them together now, among the last group of students admitted after the start of the semester. They had once shared the strongest of friendships. But that all ended a long time ago.

But when an insufferable but politically important woman turns up murdered, the two agree to put their differences aside and work together to solve the case.

Because the murderer might strike again. But more importantly, solving a murder would just have to impress the dour colonel who clearly thinks neither of them belong at his academy.

Murder on the Intergalactic Railway, the first book in the Ritchie and Fitz Sci-Fi Murder Mysteries.

FREE EBOOK!

Like exclusive, free content?

If you'd like to receive "The Cat's Hammer," a free prequel short story to the Viking Witch Cozy Mystery series, plus a ton of other free goodies, go to CateMartin.com to subscribe to my monthly newsletter! This eBook is exclusively for newsletter subscribers and will never be sold in stores. Check it out!

ABOUT THE AUTHOR

Cate Martin is a mystery writer who lives in Minneapolis, Minnesota.

ALSO BY CATE MARTIN

The Witches Three Cozy Mystery Series

Charm School

Work Like a Charm

Third Time is a Charm

Old World Charm

Charm his Pants Off

Charm Offensive

The Viking Witch Cozy Mystery Series

Body at the Crossroads

Death Under the Bridge

Murder on the Lake

Killing in the Village Commons (coming February 9, 2021)